GALVANIZED

M' ALAN B

M'Alan B

Galvanized

Published by BooxAi

ISBN: 978-965-578-984-3

CONTENTS

GALVANIZED

galvanize

verb

the letter managed to galvanize him into action: impel, stir, spur, prod, urge, motivate, stimulate, arouse, awaken, invigorate, inspire, incentivize

PREFACE

What's to know about Lazy Love? Her father is a mystery and her mother was everything to her. Love inherited her thoughtfulness, goodwill, and compassion from her mother. She protects her energy well, so she's only available on her terms as a hyper-independent woman. Standing firmly on that square, she can only be sincerely wooed, not bought or dickmatized. She's no 'basketball wife' or needy in any way. Love's got her own (like the R&B artist sings). She's a pure feminist in that she wants the double standard crushed or napalmed into smithereens. Love doesn't mind paying for dinner or taking out the trash; she's a true partner.

CHAPTER ONE

LADY LOVE (Afifa)

Love knows she's special; however, she's very graceful about it. Lazy Love may be more fitting for her dating efforts, but she actually accomplishes too much to be considered lazy (she's very laid back overall, though).

If you've been paying attention, you can see why she may be single:

ALPHAS, CHAUVINISTS, and BETA PROVIDERS need not apply. An omega type may qualify, whatever that is.

Afifa is relaxing by her fireplace. As she continues a novel she's reading, she thinks about the intense gaze of the man who accosted her.

He admitted not being well versed in his communication and that he had to know about her. He said he vowed to himself that he would not be in suspense concerning her. That's why he introduced himself and stated his case. His gaze and sincerity made her tingle a bit. She was feeling his earnest introduction, but she really didn't give out her number. Such a professional, Afifa, politely asked for his business card (because, in her mind, it would be nice if she had these tingly sensations for a businessman).

Tyrone didn't have a card. What he had was a blank look on his face for half a second before spouting his decree: "I'd appreciate it if you put my number in your phone; it may end up being your most important number. I detect the chemistry; your only issue is that I'm a total stranger, and my issue is that we may not ever know how much of a fit we are. We should address this potential."

Afifa was drawn to the guy, but she was always cautious with men. She honestly responded,

"You seem genuine, so I'll accept your number, but I won't make any promises after that."

Afifa punched his information in her phone and left the lobby to go back to her hotel room.

Tyrone stood in the same spot as she left. He was soaking in the scenario. Tyrone stepped to her to rid himself of the suspense. The irony dawns on him. Now he's smiling sourly at himself, thinking *she's feeling me, but she's cautious, and I may never see or hear from her again*. That was almost a year ago.

CHAPTER TWO

TYRONE

Tyrone lives in the Central Jersey suburbs, about 20-30 minutes from Philly. He's thought of in many ways by many people: good dude, laid back, ridiculous, a troll with the slowest quick wit, womanizer.

Tyrone was a planter (plants his seed deep in fertile punani). He had a few baby moms. He also had a few of the best candidates for side pieces, married women - they have to be discreet.

Tyrone wasn't out here wishing upon a star that he may have just one woman before he dies. NAH, he was out here competing with the best of players it seemed. His stats, body count, whatever you want to call it, were insane; he knew it. He called himself a 'hoar' and relished in the fact that (any shapely body could get it).

The way Tyrone came up was to HUSTLE HARD, GET MONEY, and keep splashing in those tight wetlands. Definitely one of the greatest ways to alleviate stress.

One time, his headache subsided as he orgasmed, so he thought that was the true elixir for headaches for a while until he was in 'some' with a headache and was expecting the headache to pass with the 'release' but to no avail. Tyrone thought to himself,

"I should've been with the one that pulled my nut and my headache."

Tyrone was selling THC-infused cooking oil to cooks, bakers, and all else who was paying. He cornered his market. It was illegal at the time, but it was his own. Tyrone grew his own plants for quality assurance, and he only infused raw cold pressed oils (coconut oil, olive oil, grape seed oil, peanut oil). His product was superior.

He also worked at a facility getting that blue-collar dollar that went to his children. Tyrone had three children by three different women.

He was the only one at the facility with a 745 and a Range Rover.

This tacky ninja was pulling these fine vehicles up to an apartment complex he lived in.

Thing is, Tyrone wasn't at peace. A bunch of highs and lows. Great times and great drama, but no true peace of mind.

One day, Tyrone was at work on lunch break; for some reason, he felt the urge to speak to his 'old head' Russ. He always appreciated how simple and sweet Russ' life seemed.

Tyrone came to the table Russ was eating alone at. He trolled him a bit from the onset, "Yo Russ, these women want you around here, and you just remain neutral and all polite; what gives?"

Russ cooly responded, "It's all good; you'll get around to them all, playboy."

Tyrone sat down and asked Russ why he wasn't interested in some of the most attractive women at the job. Russ responded, "I never wanted a crazy body count. I won't enter a woman just because she's built nicely; there are other factors involved that will damage your spirit if you don't choose wisely."

Tyrone responded, "I believe that's true for women more than men; I'm out here winning, Russ; you could be too."

"I am winning Russ said, "I deal in true intimacy, and I'm winning. My Lady is wonderful and happy; I'm very content."

Russ added,

"Both sexes may suffer from residual circumstances from promiscuity, not just women. Don't let that double standard make you think it's all good, fam.

Baby mommas, diseases, negative energies being exchanged, et cetera. So while your lifestyle is winning to you, it's losing to me. I don't want to be a whore ass dude, just out here for everyone. That's one of the things about me that allows my lady to feel confident and secure in me. Death could only do us part."

Tyrone sat there and marinated in what Russ said. Then he looked at Russ respectfully and considered his tone and mannerisms. Tyrone nodded in sincere appreciation of a man who had something great figured out. Tyrone got up from the table, gave respect, got respect, then went back to work.

When Tyrone got off, he ran into Russ again. Tyrone trolled him again, saying,

"You have it all figured out huh, you should write a book."

Russ shook his head and replied,

"I just move within the comforts of my conscious so I can look at myself in the mirror and be content."

Then Russ asked Tyrone if he was content with what he saw in the mirror. Tyrone joked as he stroked his beard,

"Of course I'm content." After spewing BS, Tyrone grimaced slightly; then he seriously fessed up,

"I get stressed out from the consequences of winning in these streets, my business, the women, these hating a*# ninjas that come for me. I've stretched myself out too thin; I really need to fine-tune some things in my life. I don't kick it with you enough, Russ. You're your official OG, and you got me checking myself.

"How did you meet your lady Russ?"

CHAPTER THREE

RUSS

Russ is one of Tyrone's consumers. He buys infused olive oil, coconut oil, and avocado oil for his lady at least once a month. Russ enjoys cannabis at least once a day, but he prefers to smoke it.

Russ was approaching 40, and he'd been with his lady Theresa for about ten years. They mesh like soulmates.

He met her at a poetry slam (he didn't appreciate poetry slams much because he just thought it was folks saying slick words acapella because they couldn't flow it to music production. He thought it was wack acapella hip hop).

Russ' cousin Lou convinced him to go anyway. Told him it'll be a lot of beautiful principled women there, not your typical 'thot party'. Lou advertised an abundance of available women, then an after-party after the poets shared their works.

Lou was another apex predator who knew how to formulate his game according to his prey. A womanizer like Tyrone, only Lou was more concerned with consequences, so he had less drama than Tyrone.

Lou got the woman he thought he loved pregnant because instead of taking his time and choosing wisely, he based his 'type' on appearance, freakiness, and etiquette (as if all polite women are wholesome). So instead of a dignified wife, he had an indignant thot BM, complete with child support right out of his check.

The scene was dope, and the place was packed. Russ was into his own thoughts, not paying much attention to the poetry until this one sister introduced herself as Lady Theresa, then she recited her heart:

I'M ALONE,
BUT I DON'T WANT A WELL-
ENDOWED WOMANIZER,
I'D BE FILLED UP UNTIL HE'S
DONE,
THEN ALONE,
A LONELY FEELING.
I DON'T WANT A MAN THAT'S
OVERLY DRIVEN BY HIS
PURPOSE EITHER,
I'D SIMPLY BE AN OUTLET,

THEN ALONE,
I'D BE LONELY WITH HIM.
ALSO,
I DON'T WANT A MAN THAT'S NOT
MOTIVATED AT ALL,
I'D NEVER GET WET.
I TRIED TO BE WITH A SOLID GUY,
BUT HE WAS SUCH A BORE,
I ACTUALLY FELT LONELY
WITH HIM.
DO I KNOW EXACTLY WHAT I
WANT?
NOT EXACTLY,
BUT I HAVE A GOOD IDEA.
MY MAN WILL BE ATTENTIVE
TO ME,
BUT DRIVEN BY HIS PURPOSE.
LOYAL TO ME,
BECAUSE THAT'S HOW HE'S
HARDWIRED.
HIS EMBRACE SHOULD FEEL LIKE
LOVE AND SAFETY.
MY MAN IS HERE TONIGHT,
APPROACH AND CLAIM ME
PROPERLY,
I'M YOURS!!!

After her last phrase, once she was done with that poem that didn't rhyme, not slick at all, just straightforward and earnest, the brothers and sisters in the building gave her a raucous applause.

The crazy part was Lady Theresa wasn't a poet at all. She was just frustrated enough to vent her truth and manifest her man. Lady Theresa was a beautiful dark sister and was dressed modestly to do as much as she could to hide her vivacious curves.

(Russ thought she was speaking to his spirit; he had to make his introduction. When he did, her first impulse told her he was the one.)

This was Russ' introduction to Lady Teresa over ten years ago.

CHAPTER FOUR

THE EPIPHANY

Tyrone and Russ started a hump day ritual. After work, every Wednesday, they go to a great Hibachi restaurant with some Saki and delve into meaningful conversations about life.

Tyrone started to truly understand and appreciate why Russ had a happily grounded glow about him. He has a great lady, and he stays on the proper side of karma it seems.

They say if you spend enough time around someone you respect, you may start to adopt these traits you admire. Tyrone was GALVANIZED. Sick and tired of his life's scenarios, Tyrone promised to use his energy more purposefully.

Tyrone strongly considered a plan of abstinence. To fill his sexual void, he planned to do right by his three offspring. Regardless of the fact that they all had different baby moms, he wanted them all to be close. He made a plan to have all of his kids on the weekend and, during the week, spend one-on-one time with each once a week. He called his new thought process the 'Russ effect.'

Giving up meaningless sex was easier than Tyrone thought when considering the benefits. His apartment went from an enticing bachelor's pad to a space ready to receive beloved young ones. He started thinking more about legacy and real success.

Appreciating a woman's beauty from a distance was more appealing those days. Making his kids the priority enriched his life. Tyrone started to realize what winning in life really is. Ironically, the only thing he was missing was one good woman. Instead of that random booty call, he'd simply 'rub one out' and then take his ass to sleep. Most times, he'd just take those natural sleeping pills and drift off to sleep. Sexual discipline is a power.

If you had told Tyrone last year that he'd be moving this way this year, he would've laughed in your face while reciting that familiar rapper's verse,

"MONEY-HOES and CLOTHES is all a ninja knows!"

Tyrone shakes his head and chuckles as he thinks about it.

"I thought the bullshit was cool. I'm glad I know better. My babies deserve a solid dad, and I'll be that."

CHAPTER FIVE

LOVE'S PLIGHT

Afifa thought about how handsome, confident, and determined Tyrone was. It had been so long since their encounter, but his presence and approach resonated with her still.

She wouldn't forget that man, but she wasn't calling him either, at least not now.

Afifa was actually fine-tuning herself. She was certainly official as far as beauty and success, but she wasn't perfect. She even had a therapist.

Her daddy issues made her second-guess men. It's the root of her hyper-independence. She wanted a man and didn't want a man at the same damn time.

She apprehensively took a chance and unknowingly gave this sweet-talking, debonair, and attractive player a chance. Love didn't know he was a bonafide mack who just wanted her on his roster until he'd had enough rounds with her.

This was an eye-opening experience. Her user was a masterful lover who turned her out. She was whipped and out of her mind. Once he got her to that point, he exposed his hand. It's difficult hiding a roster of women.

This is the part when he feels he has the leverage to tell the woman to get along or move along. This was Love's first heartbreak at the ripe age of 20.

After that experience, she was all about protecting her peace, heart, and core from men. It's so hard to tell who truly wants to build something meaningful from those who just want a sexual outlet. The words are similar in both.

When she realized this, she decided that she would have to research and study the man who received her. Love knows how much work would be involved in that(too much), so she solely focused on getting to the best version of herself.

That's when she sought therapy and focused on enriching her life physically, spiritually, and mentally. She was young and a sucker once….but not dumb. Far from it.

She admitted to herself that she's attracted to men who should have no access to her, so fundamentally, she gave up on men. The only time she even thought a man could qualify was when she was in the military. The only thing was, she had just got there, and he was leaving soon. It wouldn't make sense to get too familiar with him.

As far as men were concerned, Love only had one body and very low mileage. She mastered her own 'hot spots' and learned her body very well. Love's array of sex paraphernalia gave her adequate orgasms, but deep, deep down, she longed for the companionship of a quality man.

She was not for the search of a needle in a haystack, so Love mostly ignored men.

CHAPTER SIX

SMALL WORLD

At the Hibachi:

Well into the nice size bottle of saki, Tyrone asks Russ,

"Why don't you have any kids, bruh?"

Russ explains that he and Lady Theresa have a very special and unique relationship that requires a bit of selfishness when it comes to availability to others. Kids don't deserve parents like that; they deserve far better.

Tyrone felt like an irresponsible ass of a man when Russ said that because, up until recently, he was not a good parent. Tyrone took a nice long swig of the warm saki and marinated on Russ's words before changing the topic.

"Russ, you wouldn't believe how fine this woman

was from up the way. I met her in the lobby when I had to meet a connect up north (Jersey), beautiful woman. I even kept my number the same regardless of all my drama just because she MIGHT call."

After Tyrone described her, Russ paused and then said she reminded him of someone he met when he was in the military. The timing was just bad.

"She's definitely a standout, I met her once, spoke to her briefly, and I was on my sincere shit. The interaction resonates because it was over a year ago, and I remember her as if we just met yesterday. She's from Bridgeport, CN, and her name is Afifa."

Russ was taken aback. Could it be? How many Afifas live in Bridgeport, he thought. Wow, small world. It has to be her; two alluring Afifas from Bridgeport are highly unlikely.

Tyrone looked at Russ quizzically.

"You know her, Russ?"

Russ nodded,

"I might, as matter of fact, I'm sure. Afifa leaves an impact."

Tyrone pressed Russ for more information,

"Did you deal with her intimately?"

Russ laughed and said no (mostly because he doesn't kiss and tell), then accused Afifa of being a tease to him.

Russ then pressed forward with an honest assessment,

"Playboy, you have the lifestyle that doesn't suit that type of drama-free, peaceful way that Afifa has. From brother to brother, you've got work to do. For her type, your stats are a red flag. Afifa is a rare type. She definitely would NOT entertain your drama-filled life. I'm sure she has more peaceful options. "

Russ' mind instantly went to his scenarios involving Afifa. The conversations they had, the jokes, and the respect they shared. His controlled attraction to her. She could've been the one under different circumstances, he thought. They certainly left a great impression on each other.

"Yo Russ, who schooled you about women, my dude, because you could have them all, but you choose NOT to ball till you fall?!!" They both laughed and then Russ got serious:

"My uncle took the time out to make sure I understood what I needed to about myself and women. He didn't want me lost like he said he was coming up. He always told me when it comes to the ladies, HAVE ALL DUE RESPECT AND NO REGRETS. He ran down a lot of scenarios with lessons for me. He was a godsend because I was raised by his sister, my mother, of course. Just like you, coming out of a single-parent home, I was just fortunate enough to have an uncle like him."

Afifa just got home from a therapy session. She was still stuck on a topic the therapist brought up: sharing her intimacy. Very protective of her heart and her 'Wetlands', she mostly does it without a man. Men come to mind, but only her toys are exploring her.

Tyrone comes to mind, and the thoughts of him arouse her. She puts her womanizer to work and then drifts off to sleep. After a few hours, she wakes up thinking about him. She finally decides to call, but only because she thinks his number may have changed by now anyway. As she began to call without any expectation, her phone rang.

It was a former 'battle' (a fellow soldier) sharing news of grief about the untimely death of a well-liked soldier that left quite an impact on the Alpha Gators of 122nd in Korea. That made her think about the deceased soldier's roommate, who often flirted with her in a light, fun way. Afifa thought of seeking him out and discussing the unfortunate news with him. She looked him up on FB, and there he was, good old Russ. She sent him a friend request and forgot all about calling Tyrone at that moment. The rest of her sleep was calling; she got comfortable and went back to sleep.

The next day, when Russ awakes, he checks his phone. He notices a friend request from an old military acquaintance. Small world, it's Afifa.

"What?!!"

Russ didn't mean to blurt out anything, but it

seemed as if Tyrone talked her up from yesterday. Lady Theresa asked him what was up.

"Someone from my military days is friend requesting me. Tyrone actually met her almost a year back and talked her into existence. This is crazy!"

"Well, why isn't she reaching out to your promiscuous pal then." Lady Theresa was looking at Russ inquisitively.

Russ gave her a serious expression and said,

"I don't know, but we can find out. Maybe I'll even have some news for Tyrone; he was on her."

Lady Theresa responded,

"Let me see."

She looked at Afifa's picture on her social media page. Then Lady Theresa looked at her husband askance,

"Looks like you're swooning, King, did y'all combine when you was Soldier Army." (She hated military anything, so she purposely misstated).

Russ replied, "I'm sure I flirted with her, but it was all in passing."

He added 'I'll never front on her though; she's to be highly regarded regardless of anything superficial; I respect who she was and how she presented herself."

Lady Theresa cocked her head. Russ knew that gesture well and responded,

"Lady Love (he always called her that when he was most earnest), I'm solid baby, rock solid, and even if I wasn't, she's most thorough and would never come for me knowing I'm with anyone. I love your reaction to this other woman's love; let's me know I still get to you righteously, so let me get to you."

He gave her a devilish smirk, then came up from behind, and she instantly felt his manhood pressed against her, his mouth on her ear, hands on her breast, fingers probing nipples.

It's on.

Lady Theresa thought to herself,

"We'll talk about the highly regarded one later, and if she's 100's of miles away, let's keep it that way!'

Lady T is on her territory in a keen way, it seems. Now, she's lost in her own anticipation of great stimulation, feverishly anticipating Russ' most fulfilling creation. It's what he calls WALKING THE SHEETS.

CHAPTER SEVEN

A BETTER LIVING

Tyrone is looking in the mirror in more ways than one. Those Wednesday nights at the Hibachi have been instrumental. The 'Russ effect' has been a great influence on Tyrone. Russ even shared some of his thought-provoking literature with him. For starters, he presented him a copy of 'As A Man Thinketh' by James Allen, a short read, but every paragraph is rich with perspective.

As a few of Tyrone's philandering scenarios got extremely messy, it made it easier for him to gravitate to a more responsible mindset. Lines from Allen truly resonated with Tyrone;

"Men don't attract which they want, but what they are."

"Our innermost thoughts are fed with their own

food, be it foul or clean."

"Not what he wishes for does a man get, but what he justly earns."

"Desires are only gratified and answered when they harmonize with thoughts and actions."

All those lines were motivating. However, the line that resonated with Tyrone the most was,

"Men are anxious to improve their circumstances but are unwilling to improve themselves; they, therefore, remain bound." Tyrone tells himself, "I know better; time to do better."

An evolution is taking place, and Tyrone is humbled by his progress. He cashed his Range Rover in for a down payment on a modest rancher. It was a cheap fix-up project; he basically had to reconstruct the home.

He also bought an old pickup truck that actually paid for itself that same year. He went from full-time to part-time at the warehouse to have more time to be in his children's lives. He took his son landscaping and scrapping to show him how to earn money without filling out an application. The truck came in very handy, as he was able to get a lot of work done because of it.

Tyrone was preparing himself to be able to take custody of his son, the eldest. Tyrone's son is 12 now, a very critical age. The scenario reminded him of the situation with Tre in the movie Boys in the Hood.

Soon after getting his new property together, he won custody of his son. He also took full advantage of his visitation rights with his daughters.

CHAPTER EIGHT

REVELATIONS

Afifa notices that Russ accepted her friend request. Now, she starts wondering how he's doing and his relationship status. She thought,

"He was a cool-ass flirt." Afifa smiled to herself as she recalled how fly they were, how dope and sincere his demeanor was. (An incident happened that called for Russ to show his high integrity. Afifa didn't remember the messy details, but what occurred to her was that most men wouldn't be that honorable). She remembered the synergy they had even though they never messed around. She proceeded to message him:

"Hey stranger, how are you?... I'm reaching out because I just found out your former roommate passed away, unfortunately, and it made me think of you and your vitality these days. I'm looking forward to catching up with you ttyl."

Later that day, during the break, Tyrone and Russ catch up on recent events:

"Yo Russ, what's good?" Russ replied,

" I know what's interesting, but you decide if it's good."

Russ continued,

"It's a small world for certain because I got a friend request from someone in the military this morning. Lady Theresa seemed concerned, especially since it was a female."

"Was it an old an old flame?" Tyrone asks.

"Nah, to be perfectly honest, she was good people. I always used to flirt with her, but that was it. The small world part is the fact that it's the same woman you met in the lobby on your business trip. The woman who captivated you in the lobby. I will admit that I saw something special in her back in the military; that's why I always flirted with her, but I never made any serious bid because I was about to leave that duty station and get out of the military. I don't do messy shit like ignite desire and companionship with someone I can't be with. She's not an option for me; Lady Theresa is all I need. I definitely won't get ahead of myself assuming what else she may have reached out for."

Tyrone was stunned by the new information...of

course, his next words were: "Russ, you're basically in a match-making position. You got to hook it up!"

When Russ got home, he noticed a message from Afifa on his messenger. After he read it, Russ thought about his Army roommate and wanted to know more details of the tragedy.

Since he mostly moves respectfully and thoughtfully, he decided to brief Lady Theresa on the situation before sending a message back to Afifa. He was all about making sure his woman felt secure.

Russ's military roommate, who passed away, was a very good dude. It was a car accident that ended him. Thinking about how careless or carefree his former roommate was, it made sense. Russ was still devastated because although they didn't stay in touch, they had a dope bond as roommates. They always had each other's back.

Lady Theresa felt a slight sense of relief when she heard about the message Afifa left.

"You might as well put Tyrone on since he's the one swooning over her now. You say he's evolving for the better. Especially since she's all that to him. Put him on, baby; then again, she might already have a man. You should find out for him."

Russ considered her words before responding.

"I'm no matchmaker, that's busybody work. To be fair, I'll make sure she's informed about Tyrone's long-standing interest in her, but they have to figure out the rest. I won't be in the middle of anything like that."

Afifa is very much surprised. Russ just happens to know the guy who approached her in the lobby on one of her business trips nearly a year ago?!! He vouches for him as a decent guy; this world is too small. Just recently, she satisfied herself with Tyrone in mind, and she almost called him. However, hearing this news about him didn't excite her because she had actually started wondering about Russ after all this time and wondered if he was single.

Once Russ starts gushing about Lady Theresa, Afifa realizes that the ship has sailed. As for Tyrone, if he didn't have all of Russ's attributes, she didn't want to be bothered, she told herself.

CHAPTER NINE

THE RITUAL

It's another Wednesday at the Hibachi for Russ and Tyrone. Of course, the core topic was Afifa. Before Tyrone could even start it up, Russ began to question Tyrone,

"If Afifa had three baby daddies and three kids, would you be willing to sign up?"

Tyrone gave a frown and arrogantly responded,

"It's women out there with no kids that I'd sign up too easily before I deal with ridiculous stats like that!!"

Russ responded,

"Tyrone, fam, that's very rich of you because Afifa is one of those women with zero kids who probably don't prefer all of your baggage from the past. Not necessarily the babies; the babies are the blessing, but the potential baby mama drama. Afifa moves thoughtfully, from what I remember. She will do anything to avoid unnecessary drama. Bottomline, those 3 BM's and babies may be enough to thwart your mission to pursue."

Tyrone sat there deep in thought. He took a warm gulp of saki, sat back, and looked at Russ intently.

"You make sense. I'm positioning myself for a Queen, but my past makes it difficult. It's not impossible, but it's definitely more challenging. I still want to speak to her again. You never know how it could go.

Later that evening, Russ got with his Lady so she could listen in on the conversation he was about to have with Afifa on messenger (speakerphone).

Afifa gave Russ her number and consent for Tyrone to reach out. She wasn't optimistic at all; she was just willing to put a period on the end of the Tyrone topic in a direct way.

Russ relayed this information to Tyrone, then got out of the way. Tyrone decided to make Afifa a positive influence before interacting with her. He'd make a deal with himself to get certain things accomplished before he even attempts to call upon her(home projects, certain books read, et cetera).

With the boundaries he put up before contacting Afifa, it was about a month before he even attempted to arrange a phone conversation with her.

CHAPTER TEN

THE TRIO

These men could ball, but at this stage of their lives, they were not running up and down the court with those mindless young boys wasting energy. These days, they played three on three half court on Tyrone's driveway against the neighbors. It would be Tyrone, Russ, and his cousin Lou verses 'the neighborhood'. That trio rarely lost.

After one Saturday of balling, the three victors were basking in their usual victory glory, joking about the opposition, and trolling each other. Lou joked,

"I haven't seen Russ on the streets since I took him to that poetry party a decade ago, you lost all your grown man privileges cuz?!!"

Lou started singing the song 'Locked up' by Akon; they all laughed, and then Russ responded,

"You only see me in these streets when you talk me into stepping out with you. I must admit you got it right that last time, so right that I won't be stepping out with you anytime soon, player. My prime time is occupied in a great way these days. You still out here chasing, stalking, simping, pimpin, or whatever you want to call it?" They all laughed again.

It's been almost a month since Tyrone received that text from Afifa. Tyrone really appreciated Russ because he knew that Russ wouldn't bring up the topic of Afifa. Tyrone knows that Russ felt he did his job. When Tyrone wanted to speak about Afifa, he would bring her up. Russ certainly wasn't.

Tyrone got around to telling Russ about his home projects and this book he acquired on his own called 'The Alchemist.' He finally got around to Afifa and continued,

"...then I'll message Afifa and find out what's the best time to call."

Russ asked, "Y'all haven't spoken yet?"

"Nah, I'm just chewing on this great opportunity, taking my time stepping to her. She needs to know I'm not pressed because I'm not. I am impressed though."

It was finally Russ' turn to look at Tyrone in awe. He replied,

"Fam, you use to move around like a damn Jack rabbit, now I see how you've been moving. Nuff respect fam... I'm sure, at this rate, your story ends well....enjoy every bit of your journey, brother...by the way, that's some great reading you picked up (The Alchemist)... BIG UPS!!"

CHAPTER ELEVEN

FINALLY

It's been almost a month, and out of curiosity only, Afifa wondered why Tyrone hadn't reached out yet. She knew for a fact that he fancied her, if only because of Russ' involvement. As she lay on that luxurious high thread count naked, glistening, she let a wicked smile appear.

"This might be the closest he gets."

She grabs her womanizer and dedicates a brief orgasm session to him. After she was done, she noticed her phone vibrate. It was Tyrone texting; he wanted to know what time was a good time to call. What timing, she thought, a session dedicated to him, then he texts?!! What a coincidence!! It was just after 11 pm when Afifa returned his text telling him to give her about half an hour. More than enough time to shower and orgasm recovery.

"No need to be in a daze when I need to be sharp," she thought.

Afifa's beauty and success didn't shield her from real-life experiences that make you extra cautious and critical. Physical attributes can't protect you from the rigors of life and disappointments. Afifa had just enough trauma in her childhood and just enough disappointment in the opposite sex in her adulthood to focus her energies elsewhere. She would never be easily receptive to any advances to her. Afifa was convinced that the boldest player types try to talk to everyone anyway, so the chances of her meeting a solid guy were very low, in her opinion.

Basically, when it comes to men, her glass was half empty; she had low expectations for men and knew her worth, so she was single for the most part. Single and not settling (for less than she deserves), so how could she get excited about Tyrone? He's probably just another bold ninja that wants some, she thought, as she finished moisturizing her body fresh out of the shower. Afifa figured he'd be calling any minute now. Oh well, she shrugged.

This is the first time Tyrone ever prepped for a phone call with a woman. He usually just freestyled his way into some panties. After he texted her and she responded, he did some push-ups until muscle failure. Then, he meditated for about 15 minutes. He wanted to be his most relaxed when he spoke with her. Tyrone picks up his cell and calls her.

"Hello, Tyrone," Afifa says after the 2nd ring.

"Hey, whassup, Afifa, how are you tonight?"

"I'm fine, Tyrone, you finally got around to our scenario, huh." (she stated the question).

Tyrone said,

"Well, I find no need to rush; it's been a while anyway, so no need to jump in the fast lane and try to speed date you. I actually wanted to take my time and get to know you at an easy pace. I have a great feeling about you, especially the way Russ respects you. I want every opportunity to get familiar with you, but at a level you are comfortable with."

Afifa appreciated his presentation yet was still leery, especially since proper words are easier than proper actions.

Afifa asked, "What will you be able to do concerning me from this far away? Let's be very realistic?"

Tyrone responded, "I just plan to get familiar with you through text and calls to see if our chemistry and points of view line up. If it does, then I'm prepared to close the distance between us."

Afifa's laugh was almost scornful, to the point that Tyrone was glad he meditated because he felt if he didn't, he would've said something very harsh in response to her sarcastic response to his pure intentions.

Tyrone added thoughtfully,

"I don't know what you've experienced, but if you would put me on a blank canvas and form all of your decisions on me by how I move and not what past scenarios have been like for you, I'd most certainly appreciate it Afifa."

Afifa paused, and at that point, she realized why Russ went against his normal way and played matchmaker a bit. Tyrone actually SEEMS on the level. She nodded her head to herself and then reminded herself to stay diligent and pay attention to all signs, especially the flags. The green, yellow, and especially the red!!

The start of a blossoming friendship. This was a welcomed surprise. She was impressed by how he carried himself. Afifa knew herself too well to think they'd go far with the baby momma baggage he carried. He told her everything he thought she deserved to know, so she basically knew he was a well-intended man, yet still a work in progress.

CHAPTER TWELVE

HIBACHI

Russ brought his cousin Lou with him to meet Tyrone at the Hibachi this Wednesday. With Lou around, it's usually a more spirited scenario. When the 'spirits' (saki) get in Lou, he turns entertainer. Lou admitted,

"I had to come here to see what exactly goes on; ever since y'all started coming up here, Tyrone's been missing in these streets. He left all these sexy sinners for me and went on a sexual pleasure diet."

They all laughed. Russ said,

"Evolving is inevitable for everyone; it's the type of evolution that's important."

Tyrone and Lou agreed, then Tyrone added,

"If I could trade baggage with you, I would; my kids ain't the baggage either. I have BM baggage that makes me less attractive to Queens. You only have one

Lou, y'all know I have 3. My oldest, my only son, his mom is the greatest headache ever on everything."

Lou got serious for a moment, "I feel you T, and I admit I struggle with following behind my greedy dick, so I'm still out here humping a variety. After my BM disappointed me, I just plucked and ravaged random wildflowers for thrills. Some nights are better than others."

"How fulfilling is that?" Tyrone asks. '

"It's very fulfilling in the moment. Satisfaction, the feeling of power I have over an attractive woman willing to get into compromising positions so we can satisfy each other. It's a rush when it happens; the only thing is it always feels like something is missing."

Tyrone turns to Russ, "It must be more rewarding in your scenario Russ. You dare not look outside of Lady Theresa for comfort, and you're the most content out of all of us."

Russ responded, "That's because Lady Theresa is for me, and she needs no help. I'd never consider satisfaction in these streets when I have the ultimate woman to physically reinforce my desire and love to. I know that's what you are after Tyrone.

It wasn't mentioned, but Tyrone had actually been practicing abstinence. He started around the time he got Afifa's number.

Afifa really began to appreciate the man she realized Tyrone was. She definitely had zero interest in looking into a possible commitment with him, but she enjoyed the interaction they shared. Tyrone, on the other hand, was starting to fall hard for Afifa; she seemed to like everything to him. What stopped him from an all-or-nothing approach was the fact that she was great as a friend, quick-witted, funny, and far more engaging than he'd ever suspected. He wasn't pressed to see her, but if an organic opportunity came about to see her, he would take advantage of it. He was just very appreciative of her, respected her space, and wanted her to be comfortable(with his friendship).

Afifa found herself 'womanizing' herself in the name of Tyrone. She envisioned him a lot. She actually started wanting to hang out with him, but with no pressure, just vibes. An opportunity finally presented itself to meet because she had to go to North Jersey again for business. It came up in casual conversation, and they made tentative plans to meet. Ironically, she would be at the same hotel they had first met at.

CHAPTER THIRTEEN

FINALLY

It's Friday afternoon; after a day of meetings with potential clients to fortify the Northeast sector of her organization, Afifa left for her hotel. There, she would have time to shower and lounge before Tyrone came by to take her out to dinner.

Tyrone thought this rendezvous out and planned for a warm interaction between them. He definitely wanted to give himself every opportunity to be close and intimate with her without forcing anything. He did his research on the Airbnb situation in that area, rented something spacious and comfortable for four days. He knew that she would stay until Saturday so they could spend time together, yet he still scheduled Friday and Monday off so he could have flexibility, just in case.

Friday morning, on the way to Airbnb, Tyrone stopped for groceries. He plans on cooking for her. He also packed well; diffusers for his oils (ambiance), candles, music, and his favorite robe. He truly wasn't expecting anything except good company, but he was prepared to go the distance and very much willing.

After deciding on what he'll be cooking later, he settles into his very comfortable surroundings. He stuffs an organic vegan cone with a strain called Durban Poison. It's said to be a racy sativa that's been labeled 'expresso' of cannabis due to its stimulating and clear-headed high, with no trace of 'stoning'.The strain uplifts, heightens creativity, and gives energy. Great for Tyrone because he has things to do. After prepping dinner for later, Tyrone showered, got dressed, and then headed over to pick up Afifa.

Tyrone texted Afifa to let her know he would be patiently waiting on her in the lobby and to take her time. She came down to the lobby about ten minutes later. Tyrone was very pleased with Afifa's presence. For her best trick, she looked even better than the first time he was drawn to her. In that same lobby from over a year earlier, he gave her a warm embrace, and then he ushered her to their transportation.

He told her about a restaurant he was sure she'd like. Then he let her know about what he prepped at his Airbnb. Afifa appreciates the comforts and at-home feeling of a quality Airbnb. She was curious enough about his cooking and 'set up' that she agreed to go to his Airbnb.

She was impressed with his Airbnb selection and the ambiance he provided. After dinner, which was very impressive to Afifa, she joked to Tyrone that he should get comfortable. The least she could do was wash the dishes after such a good meal. Tyrone took that as a cue to indulge in a 'stoner' indica strain to mellow him out. He definitely didn't want to be moving anxiously in this scenario. He smoked, showered, and came out of the bathroom, robed and feeling quite mellow.

Afifa was lounging in the living room by this time when she saw Tyrone sauntering towards her. She said,

"You got real comfortable, huh?"

Tyrone responded, "Indeed, great suggestion you made; I'm in my zone now, feeling groovy; how do you feel?"(he positioned himself closer than usual to her).

She responded, "I'm fine. We might as well have a real conversation while we are face to face."

She continued,

"Here's some transparency so you can see me clearly. I'm a practitioner of abstinence because I'm not settling. I've realized that it's basically impossible for me to find someone in the dating world who would truly appreciate me, so I've been focused on other areas in my life. Accomplishing goals and finding contentment in having a comfortable, stress-free life are my focus. I admit you are impressive, and I wouldn't even be here if I didn't trust you to an extent, but I'm a bit leery of men in general. It seems I haven't seen enough good examples of men. I have a lot of disappointment in black men; even my brothers fit the disheartening descriptions: deadbeats, womanizers, and just all types of predators."

"That's unfortunate," Tyrone said, then continued,

"When is the last time you've been held, caressed, kissed with the intent of simply engulfing you with warmth and intimacy?"

She told him that it's been quite a while, and then he asked her when the last time she was truly drawn to a man AND HIS WAYS. Afifa responded,

"Ironically, the last time I was drawn to a man in the way you're probably referring to was Russ when I was in the military, but I was just arriving, and he was going, so it never made sense to even consider it. Russ was unique; I had never met a man like him, but when he spoke of his woman, I knew he wasn't for me ultimately. I briefly held out hope that he was in a position to reacquaint himself with me when he crossed my mind, and I reached out to him concerning his past roommate. All that did was lead me here with you. You seem dope, but three BM's doesn't seem like something healthy to sign up for."

Tyrone appreciated her tough honesty, yet it sobered him.

Russ is the real ladies' man, he thought to himself. Tyrone took another cone out, lit it, and then deeply inhaled. He looked at her and said,

"You are such a tease to a world of men with eyes that can see. Thing is we've kicked it long enough for me to realize you're not stuck up. You're just the most cautious woman I've ever met. Your peace is most important to you, and I respect that. However, you're here, and you're beautiful, so I won't shortchange myself; this opportunity may never come again."

Tyrone leaned in and deftly maneuvered his lips to the side of her face. He nibbled and blew warm, pleasant air in her ear; then, he found out firsthand that her erogenous zone was definitely her delicate neck. He proceeded to turn her on, and in turn, her moans and other womanly reactions turned him on as well. Things started getting really steamy for several minutes. When they were approaching the point of no return, Tyrone refocused. He got himself together and put a movie in so they could cuddle, and she could know that he wanted her, but with no pressure.

Afifa was so very wet when Tyrone refocused; his actions of self-control actually turned her on even more. She felt secure and in great company at this point. After the movie, Tyrone got dressed to take her back to her room.

CHAPTER FOURTEEN

THE ZONE OF FRIENDS

As he pulled up to her hotel, he told her,

"I enjoyed your company, of course, and didn't want you to leave. Here's a spare key. If you like, you can check out of here and come back to my Airbnb with your things. I have more than enough room, food, and just enough self-control to restrain from my desire to fully explore you. Just an option you have for hitting my spirit the way you do."

"She responded, I have this room until checkout at 11 a.m. tomorrow. As much as I appreciate your company, I want to be alone with my thoughts. We actually got a bit intimate tonight, and I haven't been that way with anyone in a long time. I had a great time and I trust you, so after I process this evening we had I may come back to your place until I decide when I'm leaving, all my business is done. I may return the favor; come by and prepare a lunch for us."

She kissed him on the cheek and then exited his vehicle.

Tyrone was very content with how he handled himself with Afifa. He was going to sleep well tonight and was very hopeful of tomorrow.

Afifa actually followed through on her tentative plans to come back. After consuming lunch, Tyrone suggested they go get some fresh air. They end up having a great time. They did some people-watching, went bowling, then went to the grocery store to get something to prepare for dinner since she agreed to stay the night.

On the way back to the Airbnb, Afifa kept it real with Tyrone. She said the best thing she did was evaluate their scenario alone at the hotel last night.

"I definitely thought about my abstinence, and I thank you for stopping when you did because I was caught up in the moment, and I lost control of myself. I don't know what would've happened if you didn't show restraint and I appreciate that. Last night, I let certain facts resonate. The fact that I was attracted to Russ and you're his friend. Point blank, that's messy to me; then I think about a realistic relationship with you.

It seems harder than it should be because of the choices you made when you were misguided in your younger days. I thank you for being respectful enough to help me keep my abstinence in effect. As much as you've awakened my body to a man's touch, I will be remaining celibate. It's the best-case scenario for my peace of mind."

Tyrone was only slightly disappointed because he knew he was dealing with a finicky masterpiece. He accepted his fate well, then thought about the bright side and responded,

"If it wasn't for Russ, I wouldn't even be in this position. I mean, meeting a woman of your caliber who respects herself. I'll end up with a great woman; it just won't be you. We both got our answers. I'm thinking about the doldrums of your first text message to me. I'm sure we met so I could have this experience with a wonderful woman to help prepare me for something more logistically feasible anyway. My kids definitely come first, so I'll be in NJ with them until they are grown."

That night, they kicked it more like friends. No intimacy at all, just respect and a true friendship.

CHAPTER FIFTEEN

FAREWELL AFIFA

Tyrone is lying peacefully in bed. Afifa decided to spend the night in a separate bedroom at his Airbnb. Although Tyrone has a strong desire for Afifa, he's fine with the arrangement for the most part. Just waking up, he contemplates his life, what he should be truly focused on, where his happiness lies, and how he can be an ideal model and provider for his kids.

Tyrone joked to himself,

"If that fine woman in the other room gave into me, I'd be smelling breakfast to start the day. She would be crazy about my lovin' ready to cater."

Ironically, Afifa was up preparing breakfast simply because she felt compelled to show Tyrone she appreciated him. Especially how he conducted himself overall. Afifa did have mixed feelings about the move he made to seduce her, but when it dawned on her that he wouldn't do anything she didn't allow, she let a warm smile cross her face; she thought, "There are some good guys in this world. Few and far between, yet they exist."

The aroma of breakfast wafted into Tyrone's room. He was pleasantly surprised. After washing up, he noticed that Afifa was all packed up and ready for her flight back home with a healthy, warm breakfast setting awaiting him. She was basically waiting for him to join her so she could bid him farewell. After breakfast, they spoke about the time they had, the wonderful direction of their friendship, and current events. She insisted on an Uber, gave him a warm hug goodbye, and was on her way.

CHAPTER SIXTEEN

BABY MOMMAS

It's late Sunday a.m. now, and Tyrone still has the Airbnb till Monday. He decides it's a good day to relax and contemplate his next move. His children finally became his priority like they should've been in the first place.

His son is with his arch nemesis now (the BM Wanda). Tyrone thought about that scenario,

"I really need to see if I can improve the dynamics of my relationship with her for my son's sake."

Tyrone was considering counseling for them both. In his mind, the children are innocent. They deserve a positive upbringing, so he was determined to improve things on that front.

Tyrone smiled when he thought about his daughters. At ages nine and seven, they were doing very well.

Once he started becoming a reliable presence in their life and not just a paycheck, you could see the healthy difference. Their mothers saw Tyrone as a mistake they learned from. They raised their values. One was in a solid, committed marriage, and his other daughter's mother was so turned off by men. She was so traumatized by men that she experimented and got turned out by a mannish woman. She tried to keep her situation away from her young daughter. She wasn't ashamed; she just didn't want her daughter confused by something so nontraditional. The questions that his daughter Iyana asked him concerning his mother let him know that she wasn't doing the best job of keeping her affair with the butch woman discreet. Overall, he was pleased with the job Iyana's mom did but wondered if it would be best if he had custody. A conversation to be had, he thought. Bianca was his oldest daughter. Tyrone thought about how graceful her mother had always been. He truly duped her. As a 'planter,' he basically deceived her for her precious 'core'. However, not only was she graceful, but she was resilient too. She learned her tough lesson and leveled up. Knowing her worth, she wouldn't do lonely woman BS. She would focus on improving her decision-making and raising her daughter. Her determination and resilience got her what she wanted: a solid husband.

Tyrone took advantage of his welcomed solitude by stuffing another cone with a potent strain of indica and got comfortable with his book (The Alchemist). Later, he texted his son's mother to let her know he'd be over tomorrow to pick up his son after school, then texted his son the same.

Wanda read her text message and sighed with an eye roll,

"Yeah, come get your mini-me," she thought.

Wanda was a bitter woman. She's been stewing in anger for years when it comes to Tyrone. Wanda was in love with Tyrone as a teenager. She saw him moving like a hungry stray dog, yet still had to have him. She thought she could change him; in all actuality, she truly duped herself.

In the other room, Reginald got excited when he read the text. He was too ready to go back home with his dad. His mother always seemed unpleasantly moody, always with an attitude. Reginald loved his mom, though; it's just easier from a distance, it seemed. What really confused him was how awful she talked about his dad because Tyrone was the man as far as his son was concerned.

Reginald thought about what his dad told him, "Analyze with logic, not emotions; unchecked emotions can lead you astray."

Reginald started to understand, even at a young age, that his mother had unchecked emotions and a great deal of bitterness. It's still confusing, though; he wondered what exactly did his dad do to her. His mother is never specific; Wanda just says the same phrases; 'your dad ain't shit' and 'You're gonna be just as horrible as your dad, ain't you.' Reginald has schoolmates who don't even know who their dad is, so he feels fortunate to have his dad at the center of his life.

Wanda has some good qualities when she's not stewing in bitterness. She's a wonderful homemaker; that's what she envisioned being for Tyrone. Not being able to do what she wanted for the man she wanted did make her bitter. Wanda still is not over him and doesn't handle it well. When she allowed herself to get pregnant again by another reckless 'street cat', she knew Tyrone was not an option. Her latest baby dad was thoroughly misguided, but he had the swagger, chips, and whips to make it happen with the most attractive, and Wanda was certainly attractive. Again, the victim of a reckless male chasing an orgasm...the definition of insanity.

CHAPTER SEVENTEEN

LIFE AND BASKETBALL

Tyrone pulls up to the school. Reginald hopped in. A bit perturbed, Reginald blurted his frustration,

"Dad, I found out who my coach is for the league, and he sucks. He's just going to let his son shoot bricks while we lose. I don't even want to play if it's for him."

Tyrone looks at his son,

"This is one of the reasons I only work part-time, so I can look into issues like this. That coach may have stepped his game up; coaches don't usually get worse; they usually get better. Either way, I'll assist him if he accepts my help."

It's another Wednesday, and the Hibachi scenario is now a strong trio. Tyrone, Russ, and Lou are committed to the routine. Tyrone tells Russ that Afifa was all that. He told Russ they had a good, friendly time and that she was more for Russ. For kicks, Tyrone added that Russ would have a dope team if he was into polygamy. They all laughed.

Lou said, "Polygamy?!! Russ?!! He can't multitask like that!"

Russ responded, "Tyrone and I will influence you positively before you influence us negatively. Polygamy is about nation-building; I'm definitely not against it. I just know it's not for everyone. It's definitely not for me; my lady is enough. It's dope being content; it's hard to be greedy if you're content."

The irony is that Russ quotes a lot of phrases his uncle used to say to him. The irony lies in the fact that Russ' uncle Byron was actually Lou's absent father. Lou's mother was very similar to Wanda; the difference is Uncle Byron was a young, scared, unprepared teenager when he got Lou's mother pregnant. The teen ran from the responsibility, excusing himself because Lou's mother was very demanding and overbearing. All Byron provided for Lou was child support payments through the years. It wasn't until after Lou turned 18 that he started a relationship with his father. Lou was thoroughly indoctrinated by his surroundings and missed out on some life-changing guidance.

It's Saturday a.m. Tyrone is taking Reginald to his first practice. They arrive about 15 minutes early so Tyrone can offer his services to the coach. After speaking with the coach one-on-one, Tyrone was looking forward to helping out. His coach admitted he was a rookie last year; then, he explained that he went to some coaching clinics that were invaluable. They talked about the nuances of the game and had mutual respect for each other when they were done. Tyrone and the coach agreed to drive home the fundamentals of the game and then build on that. These kids will play smarter and harder, Tyrone thought to himself.

Later, in the late afternoon, the trio (Russ, Lou, Tyrone) took on all comers three on three as usual at Tyrone's house. After cooling off, Lou speaks of his dad,

"Russ, how was my dad coming up? My mom said he was a deadbeat bum, but when I finally started kicking it with him, I got a whole other vibe. Matter of fact, y'all behave similarly and seem to think alike."

Russ replied, "Your dad was the male figure in my life. He wasn't prepared for fatherhood when it happened, and I could tell he had remorse. He told me that he was going to make sure I wasn't reckless like he was, and he did."

Lou responded, "See how that works, you got his direction, I didn't and I'm reckless. We are all grown men now."

Lou put his hands up, "I still can't help myself; variety is the spice of life, they say."

Russ responded, "I don't know about that variety lifestyle, but I do know that connecting with one solid woman and taking the time to learn how to satisfy that woman. The process of enjoying reinforcing the love shared is beyond all that skirt-chasing/stalking or whatever you call it. I prefer a true connection while you're into empty calories like 'body counts'. It's Russian roulette to me cuz; pass that cone, Tyrone."

CHAPTER EIGHTEEN

LORAINE

Reginald is really excited about his basketball team. He even made a new friend on the team, Tim. They thought they were the best two players on the team. Tyrone told them they were not; they just had the most potential on the team and that it just meant a lot of hard work needed to be done to realize that potential. Tim starts coming by, visiting Reginald a lot. Reginald noticed that his dad and any other men around took a double take at Tim's gorgeous mom. Reginald never saw his dad dating any women and wondered what was going through his mind when he saw Tim's curvaceous mother.

Loraine tells Tim, "If you want me to drop you off at Reginald's, you better hurry up. Rushing me, and now I'm waiting on you!"

Tim puts a few video games in his bag with his special controller. He plans to beat Reginald in 2K.

"I'm ready mom", he says as he walks into the living room.

"Where are you going, all dressed up?"

Loraine answered her son, "After I drop you off, I'm going to Happy Hour."

Tyrone is washing his car as Loraine is pulling up. Although Loraine is far from pressed for attention, it's something about Tyrone that makes her tingle. She likes the way he carries himself, and she's trying to figure out how and why this well-put-together man is single. He seems like a good father, and he's helped her son's basketball skills improve dramatically. Loraine tells Tim to ask Tyrone to come to the car so she can find out when she should pick him up tomorrow.

Tyrone noticed Tim pulling up with his mother,

"Goodness, she's fine," he thinks, "She loves flaunting those curves. I don't prefer that, but I do enjoy the view."

Tim gets out of the car, speaks respectfully, and then tells Tyrone that his mother would like to speak to him. Tyrone motions for Loraine to exit the vehicle to speak to him. He actually just wanted to see those mind-blowing curves that have most men in lust.

Loraine steps out of the car and saunters over to Tyrone. He gazes in her direction and smiles.

"Hey Tyrone," she seems to sing, "How are you?"

"I'm blessed', Tyrone says as he checks out Loraine's outfit. Nothing was left to the imagination. If Tyrone was still a 'planter,' he would've been highly motivated to have a tryst with her, but with his new perspective, he simply wondered what her reasoning was for walking around looking like a 'penis stimulus package'. He wasn't even considering abandoning his abstinence to lay her; he was simply curious about her dress code.

"Why are you looking at me that way?" she asks Tyrone.

"I enjoy looking at a beautiful woman, I'm sure you're use to a man's gaze."

Lorraine responded, "I guess, but your gaze seemed different. I'm more than a body, and you almost had a judgmental gaze, it seemed."

Tyrone explained to her that he's no saint and that he appreciates her curves, but he takes issue with her provocative dress.

Tyrone added to his confession, "Call me insecure, but I don't want a woman that every man can see how exquisite your dimensions are, no offense. I am attracted to you, but I'm not confident in you. I guess I'm not secure enough to tolerate your dress code."

Loraine was disappointed and offended but wore it with class,

"That's fine; what time should I pick up my son tomorrow?"

Loraine was actually fuming. She appreciated his honesty and owning being insecure, but she did not respect how his mind worked concerning a woman's dress (code). Is he one of those men that think a woman's attire gets her raped? She surely hoped not. She was drawn to Tyrone, and now she is totally offended by his thought process. She thought to herself that a few drinks would get her in a better mood as she pulled into the parking lot of her favorite after-hours spot.

Lou was already in the exact place Loraine pulled up to. He was in a groove, indulging in a smooth cognac and nodding cooly to the DJ's mix. Lou was feeling mighty; he had a feeling he'd be in good company tonight. It's his first time in this place he's been hearing great things about.

Loraine enters the building and heads straight to the bar. On her way, she experiences the usual cat calls and eyes roaming over her spectacular frame. The atmosphere and the waitresses that usually made her drinks nice and strong were the reasons she enjoyed this happy hour location the most. The DJ was boss too! She liked some of the attention but not all of it, so she did her best to take it all in stride. A new handsome face was at the bar and motioned her to where he was at the bar. She just saw it as an opportunity to get her drink sooner; she wasn't worried about paying for it. Lorraine didn't come for free drinks.

Lou thought he was dreaming. The woman he was intrigued by looked amazing to him. The dark liquor enhanced his appreciation of her and multiplied his confidence in himself. Lou was full of himself.

"I'd like to interview you for many positions', he said as she approached. "What are you drinking?"

She chuckled at his attempt, then told him she was drinking Long Island iced tea and dropped a $50 on the counter. The barmaid was already familiar and was making her drink because Loraine tips very well.

After receiving her drink she looked at Lou, "I don't think I've ever saw you in here before. You see something you think you like, huh?"

Lou stood up to offer his seat only so he could have her in his space to see if she was game for his sales pitch.

"I'm Lou, curvy Goddess; everything slowed down when you walked in; your frame is calling out to me. The physical attraction is strong, I'm just on my due diligence, checking for chemistry, what's your name?"

She responded, "I'm Loraine, I'm single, no-nonsense, and I'm not easy. I'm mellow, and I'm leery of your type. You seem like a one-night stand connoisseur, and if that's the case, you'll be fine. It's plenty women that would go for that, it's not my style."

That sobered Lou a tad, but he just took another

strong sip to solve that, then smiled at Loraine warm and brightly,

"What is your style Loraine? You may be on to me, but I'm flexible, especially when I have the ideal motivation. All of a sudden, I'm not concerned about the one-night stand; it's about getting you in another setting far better than this and having a conversation over a good meal." Loraine appreciated his approach, sipped her drink, and considered his proposal of dinner,

"A conversation over a good meal huh? You sure you just don't want to bypass me for something easier tonight? I won't lie; your presence has appeal, but my antenna is always raised when your type stalks."

They both laugh.

After talking and drinking for well over an hour, they were very comfortable with each other. Lou got her information and told her he was looking forward to an outing with her. He left the bar very horny with visions of Loraine, so he called a backup booty call to quench his thirst. Lou was something else. He needed a release, and any sexy, available body would do.

CHAPTER NINETEEN

BASKETBALL AND BROTHERHOOD

The next a.m. Tyrone was working out the boys. Working on their strength, conditioning, and skill set. For some reason, he kept thinking about Tim's mom; she was too fine. It seems like she was giving him slight choosing signals that he didn't act on. Then his mind drifted to Afifa; he wondered what she was doing. Refocusing on his pupils, he told Reginald,

"Don't get lazy, stay committed, follow through on that jumper every time, no matter how fatigued you are. Only good habits over here, matter of fact, while you're tired, shoot free throws to simulate late-game fatigue. Let's see how good your muscle memory is, y'all have too much potential not to fulfill it."

"When it comes to women, it's best to focus on what you like, not what you don't like. You'll seem so negative and may even be considered sassy in some women's circles."

Tyrone responded to Russ, "It was my way of letting her know that I noticed her like everyone else; I just have my reservations."

Russ replied sarcastically, "Did it work? Is she in three-fourths of cloth now?" Then Russ continued, "I have my preferences, too; the thing is, you should never let how a woman dresses affect you."

Lou chimed in, "I went to this Happy Hour spot I've never been to before and met this certified dime piece; her outfit left nothing to the imagination. I mean, she didn't come off like a 'hoar,' but she had on a salacious uniform ...nonetheless. She was a one-night stand plan, but she wasn't having it. I may actually have to take her out. You don't miss sinking your salami in a random 'hotbox' and stirring it up Tyrone? If you saw Loraine, you'd probably be back at it like you never left the game."

Tyrone asks, "Did you say Loraine?" Lou nodded in response while smiling.

"Russ, that's the same woman I shaded about her dress code, small world," Tyrone said.

Tyrone continued, "Russ, your lady dresses so modest, I thought that was one of your requirements in a woman."

Russ responded, "I have my preferences as far as that, but I don't get caught up."

Russ added, "Lady Theresa could stop traffic if she

dressed to thrill men. I guess she doesn't want her body to be her focus. It will be my focus tonight!"

They all laughed.

Tyrone readdressed Lou, "Hold up, Lou, to address your question from earlier, I've been abstinent ever since I started communicating with Afifa. It become a celibate lifestyle for me. I'm not looking for sex, I'm not settling for sex. I want more than sex. I really want a connection that's mental, physical, and spiritual; you can have all that sexy, easy stuff; I'm done with it."

Lou thought Tyrone was getting as ridiculous as Russ. Actually, he knew they weren't ridiculous; he just couldn't understand why they wouldn't want to have a serious body count with all that sex appeal out there. Sexy salacious woman just giving it up, EASY, except for Loraine he thought. Lou spoke up,

"I'm not going to pursue Loraine, she's too much work, so if you can get over her dress code, then you should check on her Tyrone. It's easier fish to fry for me in this extra small world."

They were almost done with a second bottle of saki, feeling groovy and brotherly amongst each other. These men certainly supported each other, a true brotherhood.

CHAPTER TWENTY

GAME TIME/LORAINE

It's early Saturday afternoon. Reginald and Tim are about to lead their team against their first opponent of the season. Tyrone had his daughters there to support Reginald. It seemed they loved basketball, too. Tyrone knew he'd be helping them maximize their potential soon, too. As for the moment, they were looking forward to supporting their brother. Loraine showed up to support her only child. She always tried to police herself from doting on him too much, but for so long, it's been her and Tim against the world...the only person she'd even let supervise Tim was her mother and Tyrone recently. Reginald and Tim were always together.

The game was very competitive and came down to the last minute, tied at 60. The opposing team was well-coached. By this time, the opposing coach realized that their best opportunity to win was to keep the ball out of Reginald and Tim's hands. That was nearly impossible because Tyrone had worked with them all preseason on moving without the ball, catching and shooting, back screens, and more. The person that is usually open is the person setting a screen. Reginald and Tim actually scored the last 6 points of the game, with Reginald icing it at the line. A first game win!

After the game, parents congratulated and thanked the coaching staff as they celebrated with their kids. Tim and Reginald wanted to go hang out, so Tyrone obliged and told Loraine he'd drop Tim off later in the evening. Tyrone then left with Reginald, Tim, and his precious daughters.

Later that evening, Tyrone was dropping Tim off. Loraine must've just got home herself; she was getting some bags out of the car. Tyrone got out to help. After assisting her, she offered him a drink. It was a pleasant night, and they were sitting on her porch and enjoying it.

Tyrone started, "I want to apologize to you for being overly concerned with your dress code. You're allowed to be as fierce as you want to be; I should've kept my insecurities to myself."

Loraine was pleasantly surprised at what seemed like a 180 from the previous scenario. She was still a bit miffed, though,

"You seemed so adamant the other day when you expressed your displeasure in my attire, what's your angle?"

Tyrone replied, "No angle, I'm just more open-minded these days. I'm not the same person I was last year. I have even more room for growth, as I demonstrated to you the other day. I'll focus on what I do like about you, Loraine, not what I'm insecure about. It's your freedom to dress how you like; it's in my best interest not to be concerned about it."

Loraine asks, "What do you like about me?"

Tyrone answered, "The obvious, that's why I'd prefer to get to know you instead of appreciating you like an object (for affection)."

Satisfied with his response, Loraine confessed, "I was so pissed with you, I couldn't get to Happy Hour soon enough for that mood-altering first drink."

She frowned, then smiled, "You prefer to get to know me, Tyrone?"

Tyrone chuckled, then nodded, "Definitely, and it's been a while since I've been on a date. Thing is, I've decided to focus on my kids first and foremost, so I don't have the time I use to take to run the streets and be selfish like I use to. I really use to be out here as if I had no kids so if we can find the time to get familiar without me becoming a deadbeat I'm all in."

Loraine responded, "Where there's a will, there's a way. I haven't been dating in quite a while. In fact I don't date often at all, it's a rarity. When I get approached, men usually speak to my body parts, not to me. A certain turn off, so I usually decline. The same night you upset me, I actually met another man who was talking to my breasts and hips, but he was so chill and fun to talk to, so I let him get my number. I could tell he was on the prowl, but he'd have to find the proper candidate for a one-night stand; it's not what I do."

Tyrone knew she was talking about Lou, but he didn't mention it.

"Oh, look at the time; I have to get back to my kids. My daughters are with my neighbor's kids, and my son is most likely playing video games online. It's movie night with my girls," Tyrone said.

CHAPTER TWENTY-ONE

PRIORITIES

Tyrone left with good vibes about Loraine. He was thinking about his hectic schedule with his kids and knew that he'd definitely have to figure something out around that because his kids came first. Tyrone was thinking about his daughter's pursuits. Do they really like basketball like that, or do they just try to love what dad loves? He wanted to know for sure because he didn't want his girls catering to him that way. Tyrone thought his son was coming along nicely. He wanted Reginald to have more decorum on the court and not be so easy to read emotionally. Besides that, he really had no issues with him; studious, engaging, and respectful, Tyrone admitted that Reginald was further along than him at the same age.

Loraine continued to relax on her porch and sip

her cocktail. She seriously considered Tyrone. She wondered if they could be a match, if they would have what it takes: great communication, consideration, and chemistry. She didn't know, but she was willing to find out. She was impressed with him. The way he came full circle with his apology, how his kids are his priority, and his gaze actually turns her on. She hasn't felt that way since she fell for Tim's dad. She truly believed his dad was sincere; he himself didn't know he was lying. The man thought he could commit to one fine woman in a world full of them. They both believed the lie until he started his philandering. No rebound sex for Lorraine. She'd commit to raising her son and buy a sex toy or two for the void of a man.

It's Sunday, and the trio is at it again, taking on all comers in the neighborhood. Tyrone, Russ, and Lou destroying the competition. After over an hour of playing, they cooled off with water and fruit.

"Tyrone," Lou started, "Have you checked on Loraine yet? It's too easy; her son is with you half the time already, right?"

Tyrone responded, "No doubt we chopped it up; she's definitely chill. I plan to get familiar with her if possible. You know I'm all about my kids and coaching duties. My priorities."

Russ interjected, "Tyrone, you know you come first, right?"

"You don't have kids, Russ, so I wouldn't expect

you to understand that my kids come first," Tyrone responded.

Russ explained, "If you're not in the best space mentally and physically, you can't be at your best to take care of your priorities. We are hardwired to move optimally when we have a solid partner; it's strength in a compatible union. If you have an opportunity to have a solid mate, you should figure it out and find a way to look into it. Pass that cone." Tyrone passed the smoke and responded, "Makes sense."

Lou listens to what sounds like a foreign language to him; he interjects, "It's the opposite for me; if I have a one-night stand to freaky ass ten at 2 am that turned into a two at 10 am, I'm taking the twelve step program to cure my drunk vision."

Tyrone and Russ laugh and Russ starts choking on the cone.

The week was going along smoothly. It was Daughters Day (Thursday), and Tyrone was considering his daughters earnestly. He wanted to truly know their interest and support them in what they really liked. He found out that his oldest daughter Bianca didn't like basketball as much as he thought. However, his younger daughter, Iyana, did though. He found out that his eldest was into arts and crafts/DIY. Her mother told him about all the things she had done and the ideas she had shared. At that point, Tyrone was convinced he should give them each their own day so he could support their interests with undivided attention. Tyrone felt a moment of pride within himself when he thought about his kids and how he put himself in a position to support and appreciate them to the fullest.

The next day, Friday, Loraine drops Tim off as usual. Tyrone comes out to the car to speak to her. After they greet each other, Tyrone says,

"I realized that I need to spend even more time with my daughters, making me even more unavailable for us to get familiar. I thought my daughters were basketball junkies like myself, but only one is. The other is into arts and crafts."

Loraine's eyes lit up, "Really?!! I own a paint and sip business, and I also do arts and crafts as well for kids on certain occasions and seniors, too. Your daughter is actually making it possible for us. I can definitely arrange something in that lane for her to enjoy."

Tyrone liked the sound of that.

After another great Thursday evening with his girls, he lets them know his new intentions.

"I'm going to give you guys separate days because I want Bianca to be able to focus on her arts and crafts when I'm with her, and Iyana, we'll still focus on your basketball." Although pleased with her dad's consideration, big sister Bianca suggested that they both be together with their dad both days. She likes basketball enough to support her younger sister, and she's sure her sister will like some aspects of arts and crafts. Tyrone loved the idea,

"I get to see how both of my daughters react to Loraine when she sets her shop up for our date."

Another weekend arrives. Tyrone's daughters love coming to watch their brother's team kick butt and the outings they have afterwards. The girls are very, really happy these days.

CHAPTER TWENTY-TWO

HIBACHI AND WOMEN

Lou's drunk, talking about his favorite subject again: episodes with women.

"I remember when I had this nice little curvy brown situation, all set up, teenage days way back. She called me over to a house she was babysitting at. When I came over, she directed me to the finished basement downstairs and said she be right there. She came down and almost turned me out. She had that body and that tight, wet, wet. Anyway, as soon as I got dressed the door was opening: a surprise, an early return from the homeowners. That girl wasn't worth a damn. She played it off like I wasn't there, collected her babysitting fee, and left me trapped in the basement. I waited until the house was quiet, then slowly made my way upstairs to the door. I thought I'd make it, but I couldn't figure out those locks; it was crazy!"

"What did you do?" Tyrone asked.

Lou finished, "I decided my goose was cooked. I turned on the lights to alert the homeowners of my presence, and hopefully, I'd get out with my life. I started talking loud, saying I'm no thief, I was stuck in the basement your babysitter invited me, I just want to leave. A disgusted man came downstairs and screw-faced me as he let me out. Shit was crazy. They laughed at Lou heartily.

Tyrone said, "That's some irony. Russ has something tangible, but it may be boring to share with the world. In my opinion, couples like Russ and Lady Theresa are so involved in their healthy relationship that they don't have time to be on panels giving relationship advice, or to tell all. It's always the drama that's on the front page anyway; that's what the people want: a car crash. Folks want drama; peace and love is boring and doesn't sell. I'm taking my daughters to Loraine's shop next week for arts and crafts. I never thought I'd be doing arts and crafts, but if you support your kids, you're liable to support anything good. I told Loraine about my eldest daughter's interest in crafts, and Loraine let me know that's her lane. I think it's dope."

Russ replied, "It is, SALUTE!" They all raised their saki cups....THE BROTHERHOOD.

Around this same time, Wanda is pissed. She looks at her pregnancy test again and sighs to herself. "I know this slick ninja just wanted a mind-blowing orgasm, and my drunk ass was just going with the flow because he was making it seem like it was only right. He was looking good, smelling good, feeling good, talking so smooth, and now this shit.

"I'm not having this one", she lies to herself.

Although she was reckless, she doesn't believe in abortion. Wanda's about to have a 3rd baby daddy. Her girlfriends still praised her(in her face), such a dysfunctional group; they told her,

"You know how bad you have to be to have all baller baby daddies. All those ninjas get money!"

The ironic part is that Tyrone, the one that is ballin' the least these days, is the one she's always wanted above all. Once the second baby dad entered the equation, Tyrone didn't even give her a second glance. These days, Tyrone seems to be a whole different person. The one SHE thought SHE could turn him into.

Now she's pissed at him all over again. She's in her misery and very demanding, she calls him.

"Why didn't you bring Reginald by, you know I'm suppose to have Sundays with him."

She starts in right after his greeting. Tyrone responds,

"You're right, I apologize. Reginald wasn't feeling up to it, and I didn't want to force it. Hey Wanda, I'd like us all to go to counseling so we can create a healthier atmosphere for Reginald. Please seriously consider it; I'm sure it will help us all. I can get us six free counseling sessions through my job; then, if we need to continue, I'll cover it."

Wanda was steamed, "Nigga please, we needed counseling after you swoll my belly over a decade ago, FOOL BYE!"

She hung up the phone, pissed.

Tyrone looked at his phone and thought to himself as he shook his head,

"I can't have my son around all that toxicity."

CHAPTER TWENTY-THREE

ARTS, CRAFTS, LOVE, and THERAPY

It's finally time to for Tyrone to take his daughters to Loraine's shop for arts and crafts. Loraine's specialty is arts and crafts. She uses techniques like macrame, crocheting, knitting, and weaving to handcraft fiber wall art accented with copper and wood. There was no need to go all out, she's starting with the basics to see exactly how far along Tyrone's experienced daughter is and not overwhelm the inexperienced daughter.

The girls really enjoyed their time at the shop. They thought Loraine was great. The girls weren't aware of the sparks between their dad and Loraine; they were just happy with their projects. Bianca was so advanced Loraine knew she was ready to show her more intricate projects. Loraine was very impressed with the girls. Tyrone's daughters were respectful, beautiful young flowers that were fun to be around.

(Real Love continues)

Lady Theresa walks into Russ' embrace. She fits perfectly into his arms. She's paid her dues and learned from her mistakes. Her lessons and energy lead her to the most genuine and thoughtful man she has ever met. She feels so fortunate; she knows how bleak it could be for black women out there who want a man they can truly believe in.

"Russ," she starts, "How did my poem make you feel the night we met all those years ago? Did you feel sorry for me?"

Russ responded, "Nah, I felt empowered after you spoke about your dilemma. You were telling me how hard it is to filter out all the BS and that you wanted someone you could believe in. I was truly touched by your words. Your whole vibe drew me in, and once we met, I've been dedicated to your happiness ever since. Your happiness does wonders for me. I'm so glad I met you, Empress."

This was another prelude to another meaningful night of physical bonding. Tension relieving pleasure, reinforcing a bond that is surreal between them. An amazing relationship based on team-first principles and unselfishness. That was their recipe for bliss.

Tyrone decides to reach out again to Wanda to see if they can have a healthy interaction for Reginald's sake.

He was able to get her to agree to go meet him at their favorite soul food restaurant from better days long ago between the two.

After sincerely greeting her, Tyrone expresses himself, "I want us to have a better relationship as co-parents for Reginald's sake and ours. I care about you, Wanda; you're the mother of my firstborn son, so I truly want you well; how have you been?"

Wanda dramatically replied, "STRESSED!!"

Then, from out of nowhere, she broke down and started sobbing quietly. Tyrone came to her side of the table to console her. He hugged her, then looked into her eyes and read her distress. He just saw sadness, hurt, and pain. He wiped a tear from the side of her face and then went back to his seat.

Tyrone reacted, "Wanda, what's going on? I haven't seen you with this type of emotion since...never mind; it's just been a while since I saw you show this type of distress; anger is what I'm used to seeing; this is rare."

Wanda composed herself, then looked at Tyrone for at least a minute, thinking, "This man has truly grown up. This is the man I've always wanted, this version. I had the young, ho-ass version. He really is doing a great job with our son. I give him that, but he did horribly with me. After I got pregnant by the next, he didn't get jealous; he was just an unavailable, yet a dependable child support payment. Now, all these years later, he's a responsible parent and got me out here being bitter. This ain't about me."

Wanda considered her own thoughts, and then she said to Tyrone,

"I know why you've got me here. I'll go to counseling with you for Reginald's sake."

Wanda put her son first; finally, a selfless act, Tyrone thought. She agreed to the counseling they needed for the sake of their son. Tyrone's heart went out to Wanda. He felt it; she did love him. That wasn't enough because Tyrone didn't like her decision-making. Her last baby daddy seemed so ridiculous to Tyrone that he lost respect for Wanda. When the 'city boy' got locked up, Tyrone wasn't surprised in the least. The guy thought he could rob banks for a living.

CHAPTER TWENTY-FOUR

LOU'S REVISED AMBITION

Lou is overthinking women in his mind, "I just get that box and go on to the next. It is what it is; why am I tripping about it now?" he wonders. He hops in his car to cruise a bit and considers his evolving thought process concerning women.

Lou's money was decent, and his biggest responsibility was his precious young daughter, Aria. Aria's mother had physical appeal galore and great etiquette. However, beneath the surface, she was influenced by her mother to be a first class gold digger. Indoctrinated to chase after shiny things and no substance. His BM started out intoxicatingly pleasing to Lou; he was so whipped he thought she was wife material, so he had his most irresponsible sex with her, reasoning that impregnating her was meant to be if it happened.

Tania (Lou's BM's name) was surveying her 'jurisdiction' the whole time, ready to give an opportunity to the most sincere baller with the biggest bag. It took until Aria turned almost 2 for the 'proper baller' to make her acquaintance. He then proceeded to smoothly take her off of Lou's hands. Lou was suspicious around the time Tania started creeping, but he gave her the benefit of the doubt since he had no proof of infidelity at the time. After being duped and then rendered simply a child support check, Lou went hard on his 'body count' warpath.

Lou had a decent nine to five and a side hustle of detailing vehicles. Lou was the product of an absent father and a bitter yet well-intended mother. With no positive father figure to teach him how to view life and women, he succumbed to the false indoctrination of being a womanizer.

He had a nice bachelor pad-type condo. His place was set up to tantalize, entice, impress, and seduce women. He thought he set the bar high for a woman to be able to occupy his space, yet he was only going by physical traits and etiquette.

The only woman he ever truly committed to was Tania, and that was mostly because she had the elusive snapping pussy, and he was thoroughly whipped.

Eventually, Lou's thoughts lead him to Tyrone's place. He notices all the obvious signs that Tyrone may be home and pulls up. A few moments later, he's quizzing Tyrone.

"Why do you think we came up whoring in these streets?"

"Well, for me, it started in high school and on the block simultaneously. On the block, it's simple. If you're getting money, you're getting wetland options too. It's presented to you as if it's organically 'the way'. A big reason to acquire funds and look fly."

Tyrone continued, "We start objectifying women simply by asking our male peers, 'YOU AIN'T GET NONE YET?!!' Then it gets progressively worse after you do because then it gravitates to 'OH, YOU ONLY GOT ONE.' Now it's a race for body counts, a bunch of wanna-be slick ninjas that don't even know how to communicate with women, just know enough expression to bamboozle the panties off."

Tyrone pauses and then questions Lou, "Why are you here examining our promiscuous ways, Lou? This ain't you, what's really going on?!! Maybe we should call Russ."

Lou laughs, "Russ can't relate to what we're talking about; he never got indoctrinated into the objectification of women like we did, so he can't relate to me like you can. You know I have great respect for my cousin, but he was never street-poisoned the way we were. I've been in a rut, and it's like I'm seeing through myself and the women who entertain my appetite. I'm not feeling it, I'm out here like an animal, except mating season is all year round. It's like a duality: the casualness of intimacy, a woman letting you get to her core, a stranger that she got tipsy with and made her laugh. I see the shallowness in myself and the women that go along with it."

Lou continues, "I've seen you thoroughly reap what you've sown. My daughter is getting older, and I know I'm not spending enough time with her. I just spend whatever money I can on her and try to keep her motivated. I should be telling her not to deal with men like me when she grows up, but then I'd have to explain why and chance not being her hero anymore. Now that my conscience is caught up in my actions, I know the best person to speak to is you. You were out here getting it crazy: whips, chips, and honey dips. Then, all of a sudden, you started speaking that foreign language that broke bum ninjas need to adopt ABSTINENCE. I was all the way confused. Why exactly would you stop having a thorough rotation of women and go cold turkey?!! It seemed crazy to me!"

Tyrone began, "There were so many factors in the adjustment of my thought process and actions. There was a situation with a woman I was truly vibing with in the early spring of last year. We felt so comfortable with each other that we had unprotected sex, and unbeknownst to me, at the time, I was hitting her off with an STD. Those few times out on the prowl in the heat of the moment and not strapping up cost me. The whole situation was certainly embarrassing and kind of devastating. My own recklessness, combined with how I felt about her, made it resonate in a major way. Also, my son's presence made me want to be a better example. My daughters' were a concern, motivating me to be the type of man they should gravitate to when they reach womanhood. My own 'player' reputation started to annoy me. I was too heavy into materialism. Now, excessive materials seem like empty calories and a waste of resources. It was a combination of things along with simply growing mature, just being rational."

Tyrone continued, "I have some rewarding relationships in my life these days. My kids, my lady Lorraine and her son, you and Russ. I've even developed a sound relationship with Wanda. When she agreed to go to counseling, it changed everything; there was no more drama. It actually seems I've just started living my best life."

Lou goes in seriously, "Ty, it's definitely sweet for you these days. My focus has shifted from self-gratification. I want my baby girl to be happy. I know you feel the same about Bianca and Iyana. Aria is my world. I'm her hero, just like you are to yours. My question is, how are you going to navigate the critical hormone phase, those teenage years? How do we protect them from the vultures that we were?!!'

Tyrone sighed at the question, then responded,

"The example I set is very important. To be consistent, reliable, and earnest. Earn their trust, so when I tell them something that's hard to fathom, I'll get the benefit of the doubt, hopefully. We have to be approachable and available. Fathers used to select their daughters' husbands, well BOTH parents really, but my point is it's a sound decision not based on any hormones and lovey-dovey BS."

They both laugh. Tyrone gets serious again.

"I appreciate our dialogue, but if I'm going to be honest about it, we're being a tad self-righteous. For instance, the therapy I went through with Wanda and Reginald really helped my growth, too. I was just so excited about her improvement that my own became a backstory. I know I'm my kid's role model. Once, about a month ago, I overheard my kids talking about how fortunate they are that I'm their dad, then started sharing stories of deadbeat dads they've heard about.

"Lou, should we expect the karma from those easy pickings we took advantage of when we were young and incorrigible? We never speak of their fate; we just want to make sure our daughters aren't victims of the same drama we administered. Our karma exists. Let me ask you seriously: what exactly does your daughter do or say to make you think you're her superhero? Please don't speak of her reactions to you spoiling her with gifts because if her mom is raising her to be the same, then all you're doing is promoting a gold digger lifestyle; what do you think?"

Lou admitted he hadn't thought about it that way, then asked Tyrone for a double shot of cognac and to call it a mimosa. Tyrone complied.

Lou inhaled the fragrance, then took a small sip to taste. He gulped the rest before continuing,

"You think I'll ever speak on how emotional I was when Tania left me? Nah, that ain't a player, and on the other note, I do apologize to Emily. The first girl I duped into sex in high school. I did her dirty man, and she was really into me. She learned her lesson; she didn't dedicate her body to the streets; she just became a bit bitter for a while, then moved on strategically. That's probably rare because she's one of the very few women I know of in a very healthy relationship. I'm happy for her. Look, I know I'm all over the place with all my rambling, but those are the thoughts that rushed in after you challenged me. I'm definitely going to do better."

Tyrone interjects his bigger point, "You've got to put time in with your daughter bruh, quality time. Make her interests your curiosities also, and take her on a date at least monthly so she knows how she should be treated. Aria is only ten; you have time to ingratiate yourself into her life in the best way. Some things you can't purchase, like time well spent. Lou, I'm about to shower and pick up my better half. Lorraine and I are going for pedicures. Before you start, just understand that if you never got a pedicure, you probably could use one too."

They both laugh.

Lou gives him a pound and then adds, "We'll see how much of this conversation comes up Wednesday when we meet at our Hibachi spot. It'll be interesting to hear what Russ thinks; see you later, bruh."

Tyrone thought to himself, "I never had a main woman till Lorraine; everyone was considered a side piece, and cash was my Queen."

Tyrone shook his head at himself as he bid Lou farewell and prepared to spend time with his woman.

CHAPTER TWENTY-FIVE

TROUBLE IN PARADISE

It's early afternoon, and Lorraine and Tyrone decide to grab a bite to eat after the pedicures. Afterward, they found themselves back at Tyrone's place, deciding what movie to watch. As Lorraine is making her selection, Tyrone grins at his phone; he's surprised to see Afifa's name appear on his screen.

After they finally got together in person to acquaint themselves with each other, and Afifa decided not to entertain anything romantic with Tyrone, they seldom interacted. Tyrone would check on her monthly, but he hasn't reached out in at least three months, mostly because he's been preoccupied with Lorraine. Regardless, they were still good friends.

Tyrone answers his cell, "Afifa, how are you?"

She responds, "I'm fine, Ty. We haven't spoken in a while, or should I say you haven't checked on me like you usually do, so I decided to reach out and catch up with you and find out what's new?"

Tyrone responds, "I've been fine. Actually, some new developments have prevented me from reaching out the way I usually would. To be honest, I never thought I'd meet someone that would fulfill me after meeting you. I'm just glad I was wrong."

At that point of the conversation, Lorraine looked up in an inquisitive manner. She couldn't hide her intrigue any longer. Out of the corner of his eye, Tyrone noticed and stopped his shenanigans. He became very direct, as if the whole time he was trolling Lorraine,

"Afifa, I'm making great strides with a wonderful woman. I apologize for my initial vagueness; at the end of the day, I am just a work in progress."

Tyrone continues," I have a flirtatious nature to me, even though we have a clear understanding of our friendship. I was always settling for friendship because you are a person with some great values. To be honest, I still wanted to touch the untouchable, so to speak. It's very nice to hear from you, but I won't be checking on you as I have in the past."-

Afifa interjected, "Let me call you back; someone is on my other line....take care, Tyrone."

Afifa didn't even know how much she appreciated the interaction with Tyrone until it dawned on her that it wouldn't be occurring anymore. Misery truly does love company. She was happy for Tyrone, but she thought about herself. She was still single. Not lonely, simply unattached. Afifa did feel alone every once in a while. She quickly realized that she took Tyrone's attention for granted. She didn't have another phone call on the other line; she just wanted to compose herself and better understand why she was in her feelings, especially since it was she who turned Tyrone down.

After Tyrone hung up, Lorraine presumed,

"That must've been the only woman that could've been considered your main woman before we began, huh?!! Why are you not telling these women from the beginning that I'm feeling that very important position in your life at the beginning of the conversation is concerning, especially with me right here in earshot?"

Tyrone responded, "These women?!! I've only had one phone call since we started dating; there's no need to make it plural. What do you tell men that accost you daily? You don't bat those eyes at all. Your dress code alone is flirtatious and wickedly taunting. I hope my daughters avoid your dress code, but chances are, since they admire you, they probably can't wait to be overly provocative, too.

After Tyrone spoke his mind, Lorraine was done. She looked him in his eyes, disappointed, and left. He was too prideful at the moment to stop her. She didn't even drive; she wanted to walk off her steam, so she called an Uber while she stepped, fuming.

Tyrone stuffed a cone and lounged for the rest of

the day, acknowledging that he was, in fact, just indulging her dress code for the time being; he really didn't condone it.

CHAPTER TWENTY-SIX

THE AFTERMATH (Tyrone and Lorraine)

Lorraine arrived home in an Uber, not nearly as pissed as she was. She reasoned that Tyrone THOUGHT he could handle her dress code, but he really couldn't. Lorraine always believed that the man for her would appreciate how she appears in her garments, not simply try to tolerate it. At that moment, she decided that she and Tyrone should just be acquaintances only. They had to interact because of their sons being best friends. She also decided to dress uncomfortably modestly if she was still going to continue arts and crafts with Tyrone's daughters. She joked to herself about the type of garb Tyrone would appreciate and thought about the garments Muslim women wear.

Tyrone was the first man she'd been intimate with in over three years. She certainly appreciated his passion and abilities. In some ways, he reminded her of her son's father physically, but the true attraction came from noticing that Tyrone seemed to put his kids first, and he didn't seem like a typical skirt chaser at all. She thought to herself for the thousandth time, TRULY DESIRABLE WOMEN KNOW HOW EASY IT IS TO MAKE A MAN FEEL LESS OR INSECURE. Afifa reasoned that since Tyrone is one of the few dedicated black fathers out here, she'd definitely support his cause and continue being there for his kids. That passion they shared was over. Just like that, she's done as it was simply flipping a switch.

Lorraine loved to cause men to gawk at her physical allure; the validation made her feel so empowered and confident. Over the years, she delighted in being a tease (look all you want, but don't touch). In a relationship or not, she vowed to herself that she'd always dress provocatively. She stopped having sex with men(only toys now), yet she still dated occasionally(maybe a few times a year). If the guy was charming, funny, and made her feel safe, she'd entertain the idea of going out. She loved to clothe herself in a tantalizing manner, then play coy as if she didn't realize she was inspiring desire.

Her son's father seemed to contribute to her ways. One of the smoothest men around, period. He could finesse you out of your panties while most men talk themselves out of some action and would've been better off saying less. Very debonair, Jerome was about 6'4 with an athletic physique. A natural draw to women in general. Lorraine noticed his appeal like most women and instantly feigned as if she had zero interest. The fact that she acted like he wasn't a draw and her own physical allure prompted Jerome to set his sights on the challenge of voluptuous Lorraine. Her nonchalant reaction to his presence excited him. He casually stalked his prey as he coolly introduced himself to her. The man purposely invaded her personal space to the extent that she could feel his profound presence, sense his strength, and inhale his faint but pheromone-laced cologne. She seemed to get a bit tipsy off of his introduction alone. The seducer closed the deal by simply using his usual maneuvers to invoke feelings of comfort, familiarity, and desire from Lorraine. Next thing you know, he's bucking deep inside of her, spilling his seed contently as he realizes that she was the best yet. Regardless of her wondrous core, Jerome was true to his Alpha Dog ways even though he was slightly tempted to accommodate Lorraine the righteous way(in a committed relationship). That is until she started showing from the seed he planted from their very first encounter. Jerome ghosted her, and she refused to be a victim again. HOWEVER, she still wanted the attention (validation) of men.

For Tyrone, the following day was no good. His spirit was fouled up with some regret nagging at him. He wasn't even looking forward to Hibachi and saki night with Russ and Lou. When it was time to meet up, Tyrone finally decided to get ready to go. He was lagging behind and late for the first time. Lou even texted him, asking his whereabouts as he was pulling up.

When he walked in, both Lou and Russ immediately noticed his tension. Lou poured him a cup of saki, and Russ started in.

"Don't ever let it slip your mind that we create our own karma, be it sweet or sour. Who pissed in your Cherrios bruh?!!"

Lou added, "I just saw you yesterday; everything seemed mellow. What happened, a bad pedicure?"

Tyrone explained Afifa's phone call and the situation with Lorraine. Russ shook his head, and Lou took another swig.

Russ went in, "I believe the biggest difference in us, Tyrone, is that I may do a better job of drama prevention. That boils down to decision-making. For example, I would've never dated a woman who would cause me to behave insecurely in any way. If a woman's dress code is not for me, then I won't pursue it; no need to speak on it at all; just keep it cordial and keep it moving. That's what I do. I remember asking you when you came for her dress code if it was worth it and if she changed it. I made a 3/4ths of cloth reference y'all thought was a joke, but my point was that a woman is grown and comfortable in her skin. She most likely wants a man who doesn't mind what she wears, not a guy just tolerating her dress code like you were doing. That's a big difference. Just because you've recognized a better way for yourself and are making better decisions overall doesn't mean karma doesn't want its debt paid in full. You've made strides in your life, especially the fatherhood aspect of it, but you've been a savage to the opposite sex for far too long to think you'll get instant microwave happiness.

Your happy ending is most likely simmering in a crock pot, waiting for your penance to be paid. Did Lou come by yesterday to pull you back into that salacious style of living? You know misery loves company."

Lou chimed in, "It's just the opposite; the way I'm moving, I couldn't get mad if my daughter ended up on a stripper pole, and these one-night stands are getting monotonous. I need a better hobby."

Russ countered, "Both of y'all need to do that shadow work they speak of. It's a debt to be paid to karma for moving like savages; you only reap what you sow. I make mistakes, too, yet it seems I'm more in tune with my life and purpose, so most of my mistakes are lessons I get good perspective from and not karma for being foul. One mistake I made was co-signing for you to meet Afifa. You were making progress as a father, not as much as a partner for a good woman; what was I thinking?!! Your lesson should be to entertain modestly dressed women because provocative dress codes make you assume the worst. It's rewards that come with evolving, but karma still wants her due."

Tyrone felt like a knucklehead and took

ACCOUNTABILITY, "You're right, Russ," was all he said.

Even Lou was stoic instead of playful after Russ spoke. Russ continued,

"Let's not harp on the BS; you guys know what to do to get to the best version of yourself."

Lou retorted weakly, "You can't truly relate to how Tyrone and I came up with the influences that led to our thought process. Variety IS the spice of life after all."

This time, Russ took a long sip of his drink and then replied,

"Lou, I've heard of all this indoctrination talk when you speak of your influences that had you believing womanizing is the way of life, but I don't want to preach to y'all. I do want to address your last point. The fact that variety is the spice of life. That is so true, but our interpretation is off. There's a myriad of ways I love Lady Theresa, many ways physically, of course, and even more ways mentally. Our souls are infused with residual love for each other. She means so much to me that sometimes I sit and think about what creative thing I could do that she'd appreciate. She's always making me feel appreciated. The variety in which we love each other is the spice of my life. My relationship has great equity. Many residual benefits, so I know it's right. Can you say the same about these 'body counts?!!"

That conversation was the highlight of their evening. They finished their meal and saki and then went on their way.

CHAPTER TWENTY-SEVEN

DRUNKEN SHENANIGANS AND FATHERHOOD

Tipsy, Tyrone came home thinking about Lorraine and Afifa. Afifa's the one he wants to check for. He calls, and she answers, "What's up, Ty? This is unexpected; how are you?"

"I'm tipsy," he responds, and horny. I've been wanting you close for a while now."

"Ty, you're lucky I truly consider you a friend and not another hound dog," she laughs. Afifa continues, "Explain to me how you can call this way at this hour, especially after letting me know you've found someone. You know I'd NEVER play that game. I'm listening."

Tyrone responds, "We were done after your phone call. It's definitely not your fault, but during the phone call, I was showing her I basically didn't deserve the opportunity to be with her. I probably do need to talk to a professional about these issues like I did when I addressed parenting issues with Wanda."

Afifa continues, "I agree, a good therapist is never a bad idea. You probably don't even realize this, but if Wanda is still in your life because of Reginald and she's still single and attractive to you, she's the one you should be dating. Especially with the strides you told me she made concerning her bitterness with you. You said she's seeing the big picture as opposed to reacting to her tender feelings. I'm sure she definitely appreciates you far more than the average woman could. She's seen your evolution up close and probably wants you more than ever."

Tyrone laughed, "That ship has sailed; I told you that she had two other BDs after me, so there is no chance."

Afifa scoffs, "That's very rich of you, especially considering y'all have the exact same baggage, your 3 BM's, her 3 BD's. Anyway, that's just the perspective from my vantage point."

Tyrone's mind went to how good Wanda still looks and how much more attractive her adjusted attitude makes her appear. Then he thought about her baggage (as if dismissing his own again) and declined. He responded to Afifa, "I just don't see it."

Joking, Tyrone added, "By the way, Fee, it's been reported that a smooth black knight riding on a beautiful white horse is coming for his bride. Your type, I'm sure, did he come for you?"

Afifa replied, "If he did, I wouldn't have time to

entertain your shenanigans. The man, for me, most likely would require a lot of my intimacy."

After teasing Tyrone as revenge for his sarcasm, she laughed, then bid Tyrone a good night. Tyrone thought about how attractive Afifa was, then sighed, "Let me take my ass to bed."

Lou's internal struggles continued. He digested the logic of women and knew he had received some good advice. Tyrone could actually be of assistance when it comes to his daughter. Lou firmly believes this because of the interactions he sees Tyrone has with his daughters. Lou talks to Tyrone about linking their daughters to arts and crafts with Lorraine since she is extremely graceful enough to still be there for the girls regardless of her and Tyrone.

Lou offered to take all the girls to Lorraine's shop for arts and crafts. That was fine with Tyrone; he'd make sure his girls were picked up from their mothers and ready for Lou.

Lou arrived at Lorraine's shop with the girls in tow. Lorraine was dressed very modestly, and the setting was a bit different too. Usually, only Tyrone's daughters were there, but this time, Lorraine had about five other girls. She decided to turn that time slot with Tyrone's girls into a situation that gave other girls an opportunity to enjoy arts and crafts as well. Since Tyrone's oldest Bianca was so advanced, Lorraine would encourage Bianca to assist her with the other girls.

Lou left perplexed, expecting Lorraine to have something salacious on. He was looking forward to telling Tyrone about the weird development when he saw him. She was actually dressed like a nun. When Lou got back to Tyrone's place, he suggested that they both go back to pick the girls up. They planned to take the girls out to eat afterward. Tyrone would automatically go in and retrieve the girls naturally. Lou drove and kept the car running.

Tyrone was missing the many aspects of Lorraine. The breakup wasn't even a week old, and he was missing her dearly. He really didn't want to see her because he knew he wasn't the one for her. He wasn't secure enough to deal with how she presented herself daily. When he went inside her place of business to get the girls, he was wondering where exactly she was and who the help was because a modestly dressed woman had her back turned from him across the room doing something at a table. When she turned around, he noticed in surprise that it was Lorraine. Tyrone got excited inside, thinking she was attempting to change her dress code for him.

Lorraine wasn't her usually bubbly self to Tyrone, yet she was still pleasant enough under the circumstances. Tyrone commended her on her choice of dress, not knowing that Lorraine couldn't wait to get out of that 'loose garb' and get back to her norm. She said as much after greeting Tyrone, basically letting him know that he has to find someone else to blame if his daughters don't want to dress conservatively enough for his taste. She added the fact that she couldn't wait to put her usual attire back on. Pettiness prevails, and an egg is left on Tyrone's face.

A stunned Tyrone accepted his fate, thanked Lorraine for her time with the girls, and left.

Lou asked Tyrone what he thought, but Tyrone just turned his attention to the girls and what they accomplished in arts and crafts. That was the way of letting Lou know that they'd talk about Lorraine later, if at all.

CHAPTER TWENTY-EIGHT

WONDERFUL WANDA

While Tyrone was out catering to his daughters, his son Reginald was home lounging. He had a full day of competitive basketball with his best friend, Tim, and three other guys. They were at the local YMCA serving L's to the competition. Reginald came home, showered, and sat back to reminisce about the outstanding work he had put in on the court that day.

Tired but hungry, he called his mom because her cooking was Michelin-star level. He was in the mood for his mother's doting company and her fine cuisine. Wanda was happy to hear from her son, yet she was too preoccupied with her newborn to pick Reginald up. Her second child was functioning great independently, so he wasn't a worry. As usual, she did have something delicious simmering on the stove. She wanted to see him anyway, and one of his favorite meals was on the stove too.

Reginald called his dad for permission to let their neighbor drop him off at his mom's house. For all the things Tyrone has done, his neighbor was happy to be available to assist Reginald. Tyrone gave his approval to Reginald and then let him know that he'd pick him up after his outing with the girls.

Wanda actually felt like a new woman with a new lease on life. She put most of her focus on her newborn. She felt as though her better mentality forced her to be the best mother she could. The therapy they attended helped her immensely. She didn't realize that her seemingly 'committed girlfriends' were a part of her toxicity until it was revealed during therapy. She learned a lot about herself in those sessions and was ready to leave the past back where it was. Time to start anew. She wasn't going to be entertaining ballers and was out to move with respect for herself. After all, she had a baby girl to set an example for.

Once Reginald arrived, Wanda put him to work. She handed him his little sister, then kissed her towering son on the cheek and told him to give Tia the rest of her bottle and rock her to sleep. Wanda went to prepare her son a plate of food.

Tia relentlessly sucked on her bottle while Reginald smiled and cooed at her; next thing you know, Tia was fast asleep. He put her in the crib and then went to the kitchen, where his mom was. She was toasting some garlic bread to go with his meal.

Wanda asked him about his basketball progress and his grades (because they go together) and then asked him how his dad was doing. Reginald let her know that he's still excelling in both areas, but his dad has been more subdued lately; then he mentioned the fact that he noticed that his dad doesn't interact with his best friend's mom anymore unless it's something to do with his sisters or his best friend, Tim. Wanda was intrigued by these developments, especially because it seemed like Tyrone and Lorraine had just gotten together not too long ago.

Wanda filed that information away and placed an aromatic plate of goodness before him, prompting a mouth-watering smile from Reginald. Wanda shifted the topic.

"You may end up taller than your dad at the rate you're growing." She continued, "I know you love basketball, but it seems like the only other thing you like is video games. Do you have other interests? What's your favorite subject in school?"

Reginald admitted his interest in the earth's crust, the different minerals and crystals that exist, how they are formed, et cetera. Wanda was delighted and pleasantly surprised to hear of Tyrone's interest in a branch of science and added, "I'm impressed, son; your dad and I are here to aid you in following your dreams. It's wonderful that you have dreams that I can have great confidence in as well. It's very difficult to be a professional athlete and just as hard to become a professional gamer. Being a scientist takes work, too, but if you're trying to excel at anything, it usually takes a lot of dedication and a desire for it. It has to feel like your purpose. In fact, it should become your purpose, whatever you love to do."

Reginald sighed and told his mother she sounded like dad, just softer and sweeter. They laughed, and she said that they both couldn't be wrong. Usually, two well-intended parents on the same page is a good thing.

Reginald looked at his phone. It was a text from his dad saying he was on his way.

"Ma, it's dad; he'll be on his way to get me soon."

They continued to talk, and after one more plate of mom's best, less than a half hour later, Tyrone was knocking at the door. Reginald answered the door, and Wanda invited him in. Tyrone was trying to comprehend why he was somehow drawn to this woman that he swore off and made excuses not to be with. He had to admit she was dealing with some healthy energy and emitting some great positive vibes. He didn't know that the counseling they received would slowly draw him back to her. He just focused on what was clearly on the surface: she had just had her 3rd child from her 3rd baby daddy. Her body recovered nicely, too (of course, he noticed that as well). Tyrone greeted her warmly and tried to thank her for being available for Reginald.

She protested because she didn't need props for being a mother who loved her son. Tyrone took a few moments to sincerely see how she'd been before taking his son home. He felt a certain vibe at that moment, but he wouldn't quantify it.

CHAPTER TWENTY-NINE

HUMPDAY HIBACHI

On this particular hump day, Tyrone didn't feel like cooking, and he avoided feeding his son fast food. Tyrone decided to take his son to the Hibachi spot about an hour prior to when he'd usually be there with Russ and Lou. He decided to enjoy dinner there with his son, then appreciate the fact that Lorraine would pick Reginald up from there. It worked out well because it was no inconvenience to Lorraine since Reginald was spending the night, and her place of business was right down the street. She'd just continue to do some fine-tuning and paperwork until Reginald was done with his father-and-son time.

Tyrone didn't bring the saki because it was Lou's turn, and Russ's turn would come up the next week (they always took turns bringing two bottles). Tyrone took the opportunity to see how his son was thinking these days. As they interacted, Tyrone quietly swelled with pride as he listened to his son talk about the things going on in his life and how he was reacting to situations that occurred in a manner that seemed very mature for his age.

As they were basically putting an exclamation point on their time together, on cue, Lou and Russ walked towards their table. They both grinned when they saw the father and son moment they were approaching. Tyrone and Reginald even had an original greeting. The way father and son gave salutations of warmth and respect was endearing.

On Reginald's way out, Lou greeted him with a simulated basketball move, crossed him over then finger-rolled, the imaginary basketball. Lou made a beeline to the table, ready to drink. Russ then gave Reginald dap as he pulled him in close and whispered,

"Your support system is here for you; we've got answers from all angles. As far as you're concerned, we are Tyrone's backup; that's what uncles do. Stay fly, young prince."

Reginald looked him in the eye sincerely and thanked him before beginning to depart to Lorraine's hospitality. Reginald suddenly turned around to come back to his Uncle Russ and proclaimed, "Thought and character are one, he that seeketh findeth; and to him that knocketh it shall be opened; for only by patience, practice, and ceaseless importunity can I enter the Temple of Knowledge." Reginald smiled and thanked his uncle for the booklet he had given him that had inspired the sincere recital. Russ just smiled at him as he gave him dap, then went to join his team.

Russ came to the table beaming, "Tyrone, you should've been Lou's dad too!" he joked.

Worst joke ever because it sparked an ill feeling in Lou. Lou quipped,

"My dad was your dad instead of mine; you ain't funny at all!" Lou vented.

Tyrone looked at Lou, then Russ. Russ responded,

"I apologize, player. It was a horrible form on my part. Putting myself in your shoes, the joke was wack."

Lou nodded warily.

Tyrone interjected, "Reginald is coming along nicely so far; I appreciate y'all for the roles you guys play in his development. Lou that move you taught him, that tricky variation of an in-and-out move, is basically making him unstoppable; you only see him use it against a great defense, though; he really keeps it simple and keeps everyone on the team involved. He'll only go to that move in clutch situations. He had a great arsenal of offensive moves before, but that's the one. An NBA move, if mastered, I can tell his skill will get him a free college education; the NBA is a bonus, especially since he truly has other endeavors he'd like to pursue besides basketball. That's why I appreciate you too, Russ; I know you were the reason he's quoting James Allen, moving around confidently, yet humble, a respectable young dude. That's what I got, I'm fortunate, and I'm thankful for it.'

"Real talk," Lou began, "The way he mastered that move and added his own variation made me feel like Rod Strickland probably felt after he taught his protege Kyrie Irving signature moves.

Tyrone interjected, "You comparing yourself to Rod Strickland?!!"

Lou paused in thought, then Russ interjected, "Lou doesn't have the resume of Strickland's, but that doesn't mean he can't have a similar impact on a young protégés game."

Lou chimed in. "I'd get buckets on Rod, I'm sure."

In response, Russ and Tyrone gave Lou free shrugs, and then Tyrone added,

"I actually could see you having slight success against Strickland offensively because Rod wasn't renowned for his defensive efforts, but on the offensive end, he would embarrass you so bad you'd probably hate basketball after that!" They all laughed after that.

Out of left field, Tyrone fessed up to his brotherhood,

"Yo, my dudes, Wanda has been on point. Her whole presentation is mellow. Regardless, after a third BD and a 3rd child, she's out of the running though… a no-go."

Lou chimed in…. "Wow, even my foul ass can see the rich irony in that!! You have her exact same stats, thinking you should go to the Hall of Fame, but you're sending her to the Hall of Shame!"

Lou added before grabbing his saki cup, "Your mirror don't work my dude?!!" They laughed some more. They all laughed except Tyrone.

At that moment, while drunk and heavily impacted by his 'brotherhood,' he actually felt hypocritical and silly for discounting his worthy baby momma. He took a long swig of saki as he thought about certain developments in his life.

Russ finally chimed in, "Stay your course, Tyrone; don't let these new revelations make you jump out of bounds. If it's Wanda that should be with you, it should feel like the most natural relationship you ever had. I'm only sure of this because you guys are so familiar with each other, since teenagers. Y'all experienced the worst of each other and then turned the proverbial corner through therapy. The both of you are putting Reginald first. The benefits of that scenario seem to spill over into other aspects. Wanda loves you, we know; she's matured too, a great mother. Respect her, Tyrone, and put her on your radar. She deserves just as much credit for Reginald's development as a person as you do."

Tyrone responded, "She's definitely on my radar; she's been on my mind more than I can ever recall or wanted to admit. Nice warm thoughts too."

CHAPTER THIRTY

RUSS AND LOU

Russ rarely made arrangements to do much outside of Lady Theresa, except for when it came to Hibachi and basketball with the 'Brotherhood.' Russ also rarely voiced himself in less than a mindful manner, as he did when he got a bit too enthusiastic about Reginald's progress and then made an insensitive, sarcastic comment about Lou's upbringing.

Russ felt compelled to make some arrangements with Lou; he loved his cousin and wanted to have another interaction with him to increase the peace between them.

He told Lady Theresa about the whole thing and then suggested that since her sister was finally coming over from Cali to visit that, they could kill two birds with one stone. The plan was to invite Lou over for an outing. They would pick Mary (Lady Theresa's sister) up from the airport. The plan was to drive into Philly for a good bar with great food and a greater view. That would give Russ an opportunity to remind Lou of how important their bond is to him. Lou also gets to meet Mary, and for a few sound reasons, Russ is sure that, to an extent, they'd definitely appreciate each other.

Bok Bar
Copy Link
1901 S 9th St
Philadelphia, PA 19148

The city's coolest roof deck is set atop a former public high school in South Philly, with panoramic views of the skyline and a lineup of events from pop-up dinners to guided meditation. Reservations are required. Lady Theresa made reservations for the four of them, and the ambiance was warm and wonderful. A beautiful, scenic, and serene situation.

Mary was intrigued by Lou; she found herself looking in his direction a lot. Conversely, he wasn't paying her any attention in return. Mostly because of how Russ had his full attention as he spoke off to the side in hushed tones to Lou.

Lady Theresa notices her sister's frequent gazes at Lou, and when she does it for the seemingly umpteenth time, Lady nudges her and smiles knowingly. Mary smiles back devilishly,

"Tell me about him, sis?"

At that point, Lady Theresa starts barking like a dog. They start laughing a bit loud. Lou and Russ glance over at them, perplexed but smiling. Those women had infectious laughs. That's when Lou finally took a moment to take a more comprehensive gander of Mary. He genuinely appreciated her presence.

Russ then reengaged Lou in their quiet convo. When Lady realized that she had her sister's attention to herself again, she added,

"From what I know, he's one to bury his bone in any backyard that's profound to him, but he's a good time and a gentleman. I'm sure he'd do right by his cousin Russ if you guys did hang out. Doesn't even matter though, because the way you're looking at him it seems like you want him to rip your garments off ASAP!"

They start laughing again. This time, Russ gives Lou dap and then tells the ladies that they have their undivided attention now because they'd like to laugh, too.

CHAPTER THIRTY-ONE

SOMETHING ABOUT MARY AND LOVE

Mary was an asset to the brotherhood. She was actually a grower in California, making a very good living. One of her top strains became Tyrone's favorite for his infused oils. The more Lou learned about her, the more drawn to her he became. After a few weeks of consistently being with her, he started to really consider her in the most respectful traditional ways and carnally as well, of course.

Her business was at the point where she finally had the proper folks in place so she wouldn't have to be so hands-on. Her business was flourishing without her daily presence, allowing her free time to reconnect with her sister and an opportunity to get to know Lou as well. She was grateful she didn't have to rush back to Cali, feeling confident enough to be able to stay around for a month at the most before she felt the pull of her responsibilities in Cali.

Mary was Lady Theresa's younger sister by eight years. They have no other siblings, and their parents moved back to Trinidad. These women were basically Americanized Trinidadians, very spiritual and thoughtful women, too.

Mary had no children, just like her sister, but the difference is she wants kids. She wanted to be a mother but a wife first and foremost. Still in her twenties and very successful in business already, men mostly disappoint her because she's always looking for someone who reminds her of Nigel. The most charming, caring, and protective man ever, her dad. To Mary, Lou is not Nigel, but he definitely has the charming part down.

Tyrone greeted them in tandem as they approached, "MARYLOU, what's good, y'all?!"

Lou laughed, and Mary smiled as they responded kindly to Tyrone's shenanigans.

The plan was to drop Mary off at the airport; she'd been in NJ for almost a month. Tyrone had to discuss some logistics about the business they conducted; it's the only reason he tagged along. After dropping her off, they were to pick up Russ for a three-on-three tournament.

Referring to them as MARYLOU was fitting; they seemed joined at the hip…if Mary wasn't going back to Cali, she'd most likely show up in support of the trio's tournament.

Ever since that first night in Philly, Russ wanted to convey to Lou how important their bond was as a family. After Lou gave Russ his undivided attention, the aura of Mary intrigued him, and he was magnetized to her from that point on. They started out light with lots of humor and flirtation; then, after a few weeks, they were basically inseparable. During the last week of her visit, she stayed with Lou. Lou had plans to fly out to Cali the following week to visit Mary, they seemed to have something substantial brewing.

Russ gets dropped off at home from the tournament. He was tired and slightly disappointed in the second-place finish they had. Lou was vaguely familiar with the team that beat them for the grand prize; they had all played professionally overseas.

The trio gave those pros all they could handle before succumbing to the size, talent, and athleticism of those pros.

Back at home, Russ showers, then puts some Black Butter Oil in the diffuser so he can keep the air nice regardless of the cone he lights up.

In pure irony, Lady Theresa sways sexily into the bedroom nonchalantly in the nude (as if it's always a big deal to Russ when his lady is on the scene). Too tired to 'walk the sheets' after all the ball playing, Russ gives his lady a look she knows all too well. A wanting look of desire mixed with extreme fatigue. Lady Theresa smiles,

"You want me to put some exquisite pressure on your soul pole?'

She then taunts, making teasing movements.

Theresa sauntered over to Russ to give him the ‘meanest top’ he ever had before giving him what he craved the most. She rode Lou with that dark, delicious body until he erupted with enough semen to spawn a nation.

CHAPTER THIRTY-TWO

TYRONE AND WANDA

With Lou traveling to Cali and Tyrone busy as ever with his home front, the trio decided to make Hibachi Saki night on the first Friday of every month.

It was a routine Monday afternoon; Tyrone had just got off work and was in his 'lab' getting busy with his infusion production. He truly enjoyed his hustle, the way his product relieved stress and pain, and, on top of that, lightened your mood. The way folks respected how he handled his business and craft was definitely a good thing.

He was finishing up when Wanda called to invite them over for dinner. Well aware of her cooking, and she threw in the fact that she was preparing his favorite. A slight feeling of relief came over Tyrone. He no longer had to cook dinner, and he was going to eat better than he had thought. Now, he could basically shower and then relax until Reginald came home from practice.

An hour before Reginald was expected home, he called his dad to ask permission to have dinner at Tim's house. Tyrone granted Reginald permission after telling him what his mother offered. Of course, greedy growing Reginald wanted a plate of his mama's food as well. Tyrone agreed to oblige, then called Wanda to let her know that her son wanted a plate but wasn't coming.

It was about six pm, and Tyrone found himself at the head of Wanda's dinner table, with dark curtains drawn, a scene set with ambiance. The dinner and Wanda looked mouth-watering.

After Tyrone called and told her he'd be coming alone, Wanda called her favorite aunt and asked if she could drop her kids off for a few hours. Her aunt happily agreed; she adored them.

As Tyrone anticipated the meal, he watched Wanda sashay sexily about in her wheelhouse(the kitchen).

When she had everything ready, she sat close to him and asked him to give thanks in prayer for them. Although he doesn't pray much, he stepped up this time, admitting to himself he doesn't give thanks enough. Tyrone bowed head and spoke his heart:

"For everything, I'm grateful, Great Architect; however, at this moment, I'd like to focus my appreciation on the food and the fine woman who prepared it. I'm blessed, and I sincerely thank you. AMEN.."

Wanda actually got a bit lubricated; a tsunami was taking place as a result of Tyrone's sentiments in his short prayer. It makes sense; she's been in love with the man most of her life.

After his first bite, he compliments her expertise and asks if he could arrange for his daughters to have dinner with them sometime in the near future.

Tyrone was well into his plate before he acknowledged the environment Wanda created,

"I see the situation clearly: no kids and a bottle of wine. This intimate setting is nice."

Eyeing the scented candles and sexy silk robe, Wanda was nude underneath. He didn't know she was naked, but he found out soon enough. After another glass of wine, he made his discovery, then literally ate her for dessert.

Taking their time, they would be reinforcing some very strong feelings for the next hour.

After making a serious reconnection with Wanda, Afifa crosses Tyrone's mind as he remembers the fact that she's the first one who thought to mention Wanda in the first place as the one to truly consider for a committed relationship. Briefly, Lorraine crossed his mind, and he briefly visualized her sensual allure. He was not interested in following his penis, and Lorraine wasn't like that anyway. She just seems to dress like she's about promiscuity. Tyrone respects her overall.

Her son is Reginald's best friend, and she is wonderful with his daughters.

Tyrone was home from that great evening with Wanda. Before leaving, he considerately takes Wanda to pick up her kids before driving himself home. Lying in bed, he decides to call Afifa to genuinely check on her and give her props.

Afifa reacts to her phone, "Hey Ty, what's up?"

Tyrone responded, "My life seems to be on the up and up. Things seem to be coming full circle, literally. I was just checking on you, but I also wanted to let you know that your suggestion was on point because Wanda and I are on course for a solid future, it seems.

Afifa smiled, then thought about the other woman and asked, "What about Lorraine? You're not going to be messy or greedy, are you?"

Tyrone answers, "I'm not. In my opinion, the one for Lorraine is probably the most secure type of man. She's not easy; she just displays herself as if. She's a great lady, and I'm better from the lesson I learned from our scenario."

Afifa then asked, "What was the lesson?"

"That I should be true to myself always and stay in my lane."

How about you, Afifa? Have you met someone yet? You know I'm rooting for you, right?" Afifa tells him that she's actually been on a few dates with a guy that intrigues her so far, but it's too early to know where it will go.

Afifa's vetting process is very thorough… yet at the

same time, she is reasonably transparent to avoid confusion because she wants to be viewed clearly.

Tyrone lets her know how much she's appreciated, then sincerely wishes her the best of fortune before disconnecting the call and then going to bed.

CHAPTER THIRTY-THREE

SPERM DONOR TURNED FATHER

Aria is Tania's only child and Lou's gold-digging baby momma. Her relationships with men were basically extended situations. She seemed very shallow, an attractive and classy 'act.' She has some pettiness to her also, though more refined than the average hood feminist.

Tania broke up with her previous beau about eight months ago. A month later, she's getting thoroughly entertained by this older (in his early 50's) very distinguished OG baller. In fact, his moniker was Dapper. She always wanted Lou to see her new romance, so she always found a way to make sure it happened. Most times, it was when Lou came to pick his daughter up.

It's that time of the month. Daddy/Daughter Date

Day. Lou plans to pick up his daughter around five pm and take her over to South Street (Philly) since it was nice out. Lou spent the earlier part of his Saturday with Russ and Tyrone. They played ball, then smoked a bit. After that, Lou came home and showered, then lounged with Mary until he was to pick up his daughter.

Just as Lou is leaving to take the ride to the other side of town, he calls Tania so she can be on point with Aria. Lou always tried to avoid the shenanigans but it didn't matter though. As petty Tania does, right after she hangs up with Lou, she calls Dapper to let him know she's ready for him to come over. Aria's plan was that she wouldn't be ready until Dapper arrived.

When Lou pulls up, he calls to let Tania know he's arrived. Tania delays him by inviting him into the foyer, telling him that Tania had an accident, so she was changing. Aria was in her room, unaware, until her dad texted her as he chided himself for not doing so in the first place.

Lou informed Tania that he would wait in the car until it was time to receive his daughter. As he waited, he let a few promiscuous thoughts about earlier interactions with Mary revel in his mind. She was such a pleasure. He smiled as he thought about how thoroughly he pleased her. She blushed in astonishment when he told her that his daddy/daughter date would simply be a wonderful intermission because when he returned, it would be on again.

Lou's carnal thoughts melted away with his smile

as soon as the metallic Maserati pulled up. That's when it dawned on Lou that Tania was being petty again and, in his opinion, at the expense of his daughter. In the last few years, Lou recalls that this is probably going to the 12th man that he knew of who has been around his daughter because of Tania's ways. Tania envisioned Lou and Dapper in the foyer waiting on her so she could stunt on Lou with her new man.

Lou was not going to let Tania's pettiness sway his good mood. In fact, he chose to find humor in it. Dapper got out of his car to head over to acknowledge Lou. Dapper had an idea of who he was, so he thought it would be better to present himself so he could gauge the baby daddy.

Lou was already getting out of his car when he noticed how typical the man was for Tania as far as boldness and accessories. This was all about his daughter, though, about being a solid example. He reminded himself of his responsibility and cooly navigated the situation. Twenty minutes later, Lou and his precious daughter were crossing the Betsey Ross Bridge.

Probably one of the best places to go for a date, South Street was alive with energy. Everything seemed to be on that strip: good restaurants, shopping, specialty stores, movies, etc. For starters, Aria just wanted a good seat for people-watching with a slice of pizza.

In the car on the way to Philly, they mostly talked about her arts and crafts and the good times with

Tyrone's daughters. Now sitting with a nice view of South Street, Lou asked her about places she may want to visit or thinks she wants to live. He was definitely going to bring up Cali.

Aria wanted to do the Disney Land vs Disney World comparison, so of course, she wanted to go to both. She wanted to compare those places to where she'd already been. Six Flags, Hershey Park, and Clementon Park.

Lou chimed in about going to Disney Land first. He casually mentioned how Mary lives in California and that he's visiting her. Lou gently offered her the opportunity to come with him. Disney Land is less than 100 miles from San Diego, where Mary lives. Less than an hour and a half drive.

Unexpectantly, Aria took his breath away by mentioning that her mom had been speaking of leaving New Jersey to move to North Carolina with Dapper. Aria knew this was serious information because one time when her mom mentioned it, she added that Lou would be pissed when he found out.

Lou laughed to himself about the fact that this allegedly was supposed to be a wonderful daddy/daughter date, and it was. He's just finding the irony in the fact he has to show so much self-control on such a date. First with Dapper and Tania, then soaking in the information of a possible move. His beloved daughter relocating.

After taking the South Street stroll, Lou and Aria headed back over the bridge to NJ. Lou was significantly reminded that his time was far more important than those shopping sprees he'd fund for his daughter. She wanted to be with him more than she wanted him to buy her things. This time, she only came back with a picture they took together (Lou found a dope frame for it in an antique store). Aria said this was their best date yet.

Seated comfortably and feeling good yet exhausted, Aria dosed off in the passenger seat as Lou thought about how he was going to handle his new dilemma. Early on, he wanted custody of his daughter. He had to chide himself on that too, because for the longest time, his lifestyle was no better than Tania's. I know better now, Lou thought.

"Aria Angel, we're here. Let's get you to bed. Aria opened her eyes wearily and then looked at the time (8:15 pm). She told her dad it was still early. Lou then realized his daughter just needed a power nap.

Lou noticed the Maserati was still there. He asked Aria how she liked him. Aria told Lou that Dapper was nice to her but wasn't around her much. Lou simply thought to himself that if he raised his daughter himself, he'd careless about Tania and her men.

As the first Hibachi Friday approaches, Lou thinks about the recent developments in his life. His daughter's mom was going to take his daughter south. She was following behind this rich baller that captivated her, all the way to North Carolina.

That same evening, when Lou was dropping his daughter off, he was able to have a mature conversation about his daughter. It was great until he was surprised with the business portion of it. Tania still wanted at least 1/2 the child support still. She reasoned that he should pay her that and get Aria willingly, or fight for her and lose grands in court and possibly the custody battle itself. Lou agreed to pay her half the child support. Tania's still a child in some sense, Lou reasoned; I'll pay half; that other dude, Dapper, can pay the other half for this grown child.

Mary adored Lou's daughter. She just knew that Aria would be a great big sister to any children she had with Lou.

At this point, they were in a challenging yet rewarding long-distance relationship. They did have plans to coexist under one roof in the near future. A move to Cali was the official plan. Mary wanted to invest financially in Lou's vision. A car detailing service in Cali was the plan. She invested 50% into it because Lou already had a small nest egg to utilize towards his business endeavors.

Lou told Mary sincerely,

"First of all, I'm delighted that my daughter really loves being around you. Second and just as important, I thank you sincerely for coming into my life so I can show my daughter EXACTLY how she should be loved in her adulthood. You inspire me to be that guy who embodies what she should prefer in a mate. I really don't want knuckleheads at my door asking about my daughter. Our example is critical. I don't need much motivation to love you, but my daughter's eyes on us are an added layer of motivation to be great to you."

Lou was truly enamored by this woman.

CHAPTER THIRTY-FOUR

TO THE WEST

Tyrone and Wanda were determined to have a healthy and loving relationship. They took the type of precautions that usually help. They went to couples counseling and saw a marriage therapist monthly. Truly committed, they wanted to get it right.

The environment they lived in was nice, but the scene was getting old. They wanted to uproot. When Lou spoke about his situation, mentioning the opportunities that are in Cali, Tyrone spoke to Wanda about California. She thought it was a great idea. Wanda has always wanted to operate a food truck with her awe-inspiring dishes. Tyrone would have certain 'infused' items available as well.

Tyrone's kids were not too happy about the decision to move. His daughters and Reginald had mostly disdain for the idea. Tyrone let his daughters know that he was making arrangements for them to spend some holidays with him, and he wouldn't let a month pass without visiting them. Plus, Lorraine was still going to keep her routine with them. Then he let them know about the benefits of having access to both coasts and how instrumental it can be to broaden your horizons.

With Reginald, Tyrone had a man-to-young-man talk with him.

"Son, trust me, I get it. Your roots are deep here. You have built quite a reputation as a student/athlete. All your friends are here, and you appreciate the familiarity, but what happens when you go off to college? I'll tell you, the same that will happen on this move to Cali. You'll adjust, and everything will be fine. Consider this move as a dry run for college adjustments. I won't be with you in college, but for this Cali move, I can be your training wheels. I'm sure you're thinking that I'm separating the best high school backcourt on the East Coast, but I'm really excited to see you make a similar impact in Cali. That will give us both more confidence in your transition to college. You and Tim can and will definitely be able to keep in touch. When I visit the East Coast monthly, if it doesn't conflict with your studies and practice, you'll always be welcome to travel with me. Reginald digested his dad's words and warmed up to the points that were made. After a short spell of considering his father's logic, Reginald welcomed the challenge.

CHAPTER THIRTY-FIVE

ONE LAST SAKI

"It's going to be different in Jersey now that all your friends are migrating to Cali."

Russ responded, "Right, and your sister is the catalyst. I didn't see this coming, but I'm happy for my Brotherhood. You and I will be fine, too, because this is the time in our lives we're traveling more, especially to California. I thought Lou and Mary would have an attraction to each other, but I didn't know the extent. I couldn't have thought of a better scenario myself. Lou brought me to you; then we introduced him to your sister. I think Lou will do well, and I'm sure Tyrone and Wanda will be a big deal in Cali, too.

Lady T trolled her man and said, "I agree introducing Lou to my sister definitely made up for the lousy joke you made."

Lady Theresa then suddenly swooped down on her man and passionately bit into his neck while reaching for his manhood before he could even begin to feel any type of way about being reminded of his wack joke. He was now focused on showing Lady T his usual passionate vigor as he prepared to 'walk the sheets.'

Russ awoke from the short nap he took after that wonderful session with his wife. He had just enough time to get himself together. Lou was picking Russ up and dropping Mary off to hang with her sister(Lady Theresa). One last Hibachi night before Tyrone takes his family west. Lou and Mary were visiting Jersey for the week. They had events planned with Russ and Theresa during their stay.

It was Friday night, and the trio was in great spirits. Tyrone shared his thoughts, "This is the last time we'll be in here for a while…a toast to the good times!"

They clanked their saki cups together to toast their evening.

Russ asked, "What time are you guys leaving in the morning?"

Tyrone turned his move into a cross-country road trip. The way Noah prepared for the flood is what came to mind when Tyrone thought about how much work he put in to prepare for the trip. He was even able to bring his daughters on the road trip since it was summertime and school was out. The girls would fly back home once they reached their Cali destination. "We'll leave around sunrise. We get to take our time and see the country as we venture west. I want to maximize this experience."

Russ thought about it. It would be nice to join them for that adventure if it was just the adults. Tyrone and Wanda were bringing five kids along. Russ wanted to take a moment to share some basic, sound advice for Tyrone and Lou. They are in committed relationships now, and that's quite an adjustment from being selfish players.

"Team decisions are all you should make now. Especially when your other half is not around. Always have your mate in mind. It helps you make the right decisions and keep the relationship healthy. There is no I in the team, but there are rewards to enjoy and challenges as well. Clear communication and listening skills are more important than ever."

Normally animated, Lou was quiet and reflective. This is the most content he has ever been with his life, and he is very appreciative. Lou felt blessed to have this brotherhood, custody of his daughter, a wonderful lady to love, and the fact that his present life is very nice, with the future looking promising.

Tyrone had one more thing to say. "I'm not going to make light of it and play it cool. You're a very big deal Russ. I remember how this journey started for me. I was out here getting big stats that I thought mattered. Meanwhile, every anniversary was a championship year for you Russ. While I was greedily stalking money and women, you was with Lady Theresa pair bonding and winning. I was GALVANIZED by your example of happiness. Lou, as well. Now look at us, captains of our own winning teams. A toast to Russ and a toast to us!"

Their night was winding down. The trio heads out of the restaurant, each looking forward to an intimate evening with their significant other. The future seemed bright for them all.

www.ingramcontent.com/pod-product-compliance
Lightning Source LLC
LaVergne TN
LVHW091051150826
845673LV00002B/540

* 9 7 8 9 6 5 5 7 8 9 8 4 3 *